FURY OF ISOLATION

COREENE CALLAHAN

0 9 8 7 6 5 4 3 2 1

Raise a glass to River House, the place that feeds my creative soul.

Thanks M&D for letting me set up shop and stay awhile.

1

SAVANNAH, GEORGIA

T-minus seven days

Her cell phone rang, dragging Cate Biscayne from a fitful sleep.

Tangled in the top sheet, sprawled in the center of the double bed in her crappy studio apartment, she raised the cotton edge just enough to see. Her gaze cut to the milk crate doubling as her nightstand. Red digits on the alarm clock read 6:03 a.m.

Ringer set to low, her phone chirped again.

Unearthing her head from cotton cling, she shifted across the mattress in the near dark. The glow of the screen showed her the way, spilling blue light over lopsided candles mired in puddled wax on the waffled top of her makeshift bedside table. Up on her elbow, she reached for her phone. Cool to the touch, the new Samsung settled in her hand. A gift. From him. The package had arrived almost a month ago. After their first contact. After she'd heard his voice for the very first time.

She smiled as time ticked over.

6:04 a.m.

Late.

He was four minutes late. Not something that had ever happened before. Not once in the weeks she'd been answering his calls. In secret. On the down-low. All very hush-hush.

Her sister would never approve.

She didn't plan on telling her.

The early-morning calls had become her lifeline. The only port in her storm. And right now, after months of upheaval, Cate needed to hear his voice more than she wanted to be safe. Which left just one thing to do—ignore her sister's advice and reach for the security he offered. Starting her day with him in her ear was worth the risk. Any risk. Everything. Even if it meant she lost her life in the end.

Some secrets, after all, were meant to be kept.

And sometimes, big sisters didn't need to know.

2

CAIRNGORMS MOUNTAINS—WEST OF ABERDEEN, SCOTLAND

T-minus three days

The night began as it always did, with him waiting in the weeds. Or as tonight would have it, hanging off the side of a cliff in dragon form. Nothing new for him. He enjoyed the high places. Spent most of his time soaring in open skies along the Cairngorms, playing in vicious updrafts between jagged mountain peaks.

Tonight, however, didn't count as one of the highlights.

What started out as a brilliant plan had gone to hell, bringing whole new levels of frustration.

Claws curled deep in rock crevices, Rannock rechecked his position. Right out in the open. Completely visible. A sitting duck as he climbed the craggy outcropping. The hard ridges of his interlocking dragon skin brushed over uneven stone. The clicking scrape-and-claw rolled into the canyon, echoing into high and low places.

Places he'd spend his youth exploring.

Place he knew by heart and loved more with each passing year.

Places he now hunted the enemy. Males who had

no business flying over territory he and his pack protected.

With a growl, he ripped a chunk of rock off the mountainside. Stone shrieked against his battle-sharpened claws. He tossed the boulder over his shoulder and, swinging his spiked tail like a baseball bat, hammered it with the barbed tip. Hard swing. Solid strike. A home run by any standards as the shattered mess sailed into the chasm.

Rannock grinned as shrapnel slammed against the cliff on the other side of the canyon. Rock exploded into smaller pieces. Shale rained down. He didn't bother to quiet the cacophony. The whole point was to be heard. Tracked. Targeted. And attacked.

A suicide mission, some might say.

Rannock didn't agree.

After weeks with little to show for the hunt, he was done waiting. Forget caution. Toss the usual strategies into the nearest trash compactor. A new approach was needed, and putting a bull's-eye on his shiny hide seemed the best way to get the results he wanted—blood on his claws and the sound of rogue dragons screaming.

Angling his scales, he used the high-polish metallic surface like a mirror. Moonlight struck the bronze spikes riding along his spine. Light beamed through the darkness, acting like spotlights as fast-moving clouds opened and closed.

Moving at a steady clip, Rannock kept the glow-show going. He climbed up a sheer rockface, then over another ridge. As he stepped onto the ledge at the top of the rise, snow whipped off high peaks, dusting him with flurries. The icy swirl melted on contact, making him glisten against dark rock.

Excellent.

Now he was even more visible. A shining beacon of come-and-get-me.

He suppressed the urge to cross his fingers. Stupidity wouldn't help him. Nothing short of a bone-grinding brawl would, but...

It seemed unlikely.

The enemy pack never engaged.

A normal Dragonkind warrior would've taken the bait by now. Mark him as an easy target. Attempt to blow him off his perch. Call it a night and head for home. *If only*. *For freaking once.*

Lamenting the rogue's strategy, Rannock shook his head. The Danes didn't play by the rules, never mind conduct business in normal ways. *Normal* had flown the coop when the bastards invaded Scottish territory, then all but disappeared.

The vanishing act sucked.

For him, sure, but also for his brothers-in-arms.

An aggressive group, his packmates enjoyed a good fight as much as he did. The whole thing was bizarre. Grizgunn's refusal to allow his pack to engage turned a simple mission into a difficult one. Had Rannock been able to find the idiots, the bastards would already be gone. Crushed beneath his paws. Ripped to shreds by his claws. Nothing but dragon ash dusted over inhospitable mountaintops. Instead, he suffered through boring nights with no one to fight while struggling to understand the enemy's end game.

Gaze on the valley below, Rannock tilted his head and refined the search parameters. The tips of his horns tingled as his sonar pinged, dragging a net across the sky. The signal whiplashed. Information came back like a boomerang.

He bared his tri-pointed fangs.

Six Danes flew around the periphery. Two full

fighting triangles watched him from afar, skimming over the end of a far-flung mountain spire. Less than three miles away. Close enough for him to detect, too far away for him to do much about it. The second he moved into a more aggressive position, the rogues would bug out and deny him the fight he craved.

Why?

No bloody clue.

The moment the Danes flew into his territory, the odd games began. The weird tactics threatened his control. After weeks of nothing, he felt the pressure building inside his head. The headache throbbed behind his left eye, annoying him as he continued to provoke the males lighting up his radar. His disrespectful stance should've provoked a response. Made the least patient warrior in their group say screw the rules and attack, but...

Nothing.

No progress on the arsehole infestation front.

"Bloody hell," he growled, as the ache behind his eye intensified.

It really shouldn't be this difficult.

Too bad Grizgunn (commander of the Danish pack) didn't care what he thought. The bastard never fell into Rannock's traps. He kept his warriors on a tight leash. "Hunt and peck" seemed to be the plan *du jour*. Fly in, attack villages under the Scottish pack's protection, then disappear into mist.

Dishonorable conduct at its brashest. Evasion at its deadliest.

Why the bastards bothered to hurt humans was anyone's guess. It wasn't normal. Was, in point of fact, counterproductive.

Rannock frowned. Most Dragonkind avoided humans. Not an ironclad rule. More of a suggestion. One that ensured the survival of their species.

Staying hidden, and off the human military complex's radar, was key to Dragonkind's continued good health. The system had worked for centuries. No need for anything to change. So Grizgunn killing humans—females more often than not—didn't make any sense.

After being cursed by the Goddess of All Things, Dragonkind's ability to connect to the Meridian—the electrostatic bands ringing the planet, source of all living things—lay shattered. No hope of the connection ever being repaired. If not for human females, his kind would starve to death. Being skin-to-skin with a female allowed a male to enter the stream and absorb the energy he required to stay healthy and strong. A necessary process, vital to his species.

Which led him back to the original question. Why the hell were the Danes targeting human females?

Eyes on the night sky, Rannock growled. Liquid bronze puffed from his nostrils, then turned to metal flecks in the air. Surrounded by glittering blowback, he leapt from one ledge to another. His claws punched through solid rock. The scrape and claw echoed. Shale rattled down the cliff. Rock smashed into rock. As sound ricocheted, bouncing around the canyon, sailing into the vale beyond, he called on his magic.

Ions in his blood sparked, amplifying his unique bio-signature. The signal throbbed around him, then rushed over the Cairngorms, painting a bigger target on his hide. A blatant show of disrespect, one most Dragonkind warriors would refuse to abide. Only an arrogant male unmasked so completely, sending the message that he believed himself unbeatable. Invincible. Better —stronger, faster, smarter—than those hunting him.

A smart male would shut it down. Smother the signal. Conjure a cloaking spell and get out of the area.

Crouched on a high ridge, Rannock send out another ping instead. Dragon senses aligned, powerful magic frothing, he waited for a reaction, for a sign that signaled imminent attack. For the stalemate to be over. Nothing came back. No show of aggression. Zero movement at the three-mile marker. Just the provocation of a pack that had no intention of giving him what he wanted—claw-to-claw combat, the chance to rip into rogue flesh and break enemy bones.

Wings tucked tight to his sides, he stayed at it, allowing the tips of his razor-sharp claws to click against uneven stone. The wind whistled against the deep crevices, moaning over jagged mountaintops. His gaze cut to the ground. A nineteen-hundred-foot drop.

The urge to let go and tumble into free fall twisted through him. After hours of climbing, somersaulting into the void would feel good. The release, the rise to flight, would soothe the disquiet crawling beneath his scales. Inaction didn't suit him. He needed to stay busy, was built to hunt and kill. And when he wasn't doing that, he spent time inside his hangar, rebuilding the helicopters he sold to private buyers all over the world.

Though he should probably tack a second item to the list. The she-devil—Cate Biscayne.

A female he'd never met, but spoke to every single day.

Clenching his teeth, Rannock stopped climbing. Unease chased a shiver down his spine. His spikes rattled, throwing glowing streaks across the night sky as he closed his eyes. Goddess, her voice. Sultry. Sweet. On the upward curve of melodic. So soothing she helped him drop into a deep sleep every day. Which made him a first-class fool—a male who turned his back on *right* in favor of tumbling straight into *wrong*.

He should've broken off contact weeks ago, after his first conversation with her. A complete accident on his part. He'd answered a phone he should've left in its cradle. But answer he had, and now he was screwed. So addicted to the sound of her voice, he'd forgotten an indisputable fact—no matter how hard he worked to ignore the truth, Rannock knew he wasn't good enough for her.

He wasn't a worthy male.

The nightmare he lived with Heather was proof enough of that.

Hopping over an outcropping, Rannock landed on a narrow shelf and, dragging his mind from the female he longed to touch, but never would, got back on track.

Head low, night vision sharp, he sent another ping rocketing over the range. A stronger challenge. More aggressive, less inviting. The equivalent of a Dragonkind warrior calling another a coward from a long way away. The signal echoed inside his head. Nothing came back. No return volley from the enemy pack. No movement in the distance.

Resigned to his fate, Rannock fired up mind-speak. Magic knifed through his veins, then funneled into a crackling hiss. Breaking radio silence, he spoke into the void. *"Got nothing, lads. The Danes ghosted the second I flew in."*

"Playing keep-away with me here tae," Kruger said, voice full of gravel, conveying supreme annoyance. A bad sign. Of all his packmates, the male was the most even-keeled. It took a lot to make Kruger angry, but once past the tipping point, he went from zero to sixty

in a millisecond, losing all calm. *"The yellow-bellied bastards."*

"So much for using you and Kruger as bait," Cyprus said, frustration in every syllable.

Rannock grunted, feeling his commander's pain. *"Should've worked."*

"Didnae," Levin said, frosty tone clipped, ice dragon attitude coming through the line.

"No shite, Captain Obvious," Rannock said, frowning so hard his forehead hurt. Pain bloomed behind his eye, moving from annoying ache to hardcore gnaw. Gaze trained on the jagged peak overhead, he ignored the discomfort and started toward the summit. Pebbles tumbled, pinging off the outcropping before bouncing over the edge and disappearing into the gloom. *"I'm alone out here. Easy pickings. No way the bastards should've run the second I flew into range."*

"Mayhap." Positioned to the north, long grass rustled as Wallaig moved through the grasslands. No click of claws on frozen ground. No bio-signal detected. Just the soft rush of scales in a farmer's field from miles away. Kind of eerie. Weirdly reassuring as Rannock listened to his pack's first-in-command navigate terrain occupied by humans north of the Cairngorms. *"The bastards might not be able tae detect us, but they know we'd never leave one of our own unprotected. Not difficult tae guess the rest of us are waiting outside the three-mile marker, ready for the arseholes tae attack. They arenae that stupid."*

Vyroth sighed. *"If only wishing made it so. Would make things easier."*

"A lot more fun, too," Tempel muttered, American accent flat with impatience. *"I haven't gotten my claws bloody in weeks."*

Cyprus blew out a long breath. "*We need a new plan.*"

"This *was the new plan,*" Tydrin said, fire hissing through mind-speak.

"*All right, then,*" Cyprus said. "*A better one. Almost three months of this bullshite. Three bloody months we're out here, hunting Danes, without results. I'm tired of chasing the arseholes around our island. I want the bastards dead, but more, I want tae know what's going on. Grizgunn wants our territory, but refuses tae fight for it. There's a bigger game afoot. I donnae like it.*"

"*You think Rodin's got enough balls?*" Rannock asked, returning to a familiar argument... to an ever-present suspicion. No one wanted to believe it, but facts kept stacking up, pointing to the possibility. "*Is the Archguard really that far gone?*"

"*Probably,*" Tydrin growled.

"*No doubt,*" Vyroth muttered.

"*Could be,*" Wallaig said, sounding pissed off. "*Rodin's a slippery bastard. Power plays are part of his make-up... as natural tae him as breathing. He's bold enough tae mess with the Nightfury pack, so I donnae think the arsehole has any lines he willnae cross.*"

Cyprus snarled. "*He needs help finding boundaries, I'm happy tae provide him clear guidelines. Bloody ones.*"

"*I'll send out feelers,*" Levin said, pivoting toward his wheelhouse—the gathering of intel by way of clever interrogation and the brutal twisting of arms. "*Get in touch with my contacts in Prague. See what's in the air.*"

"*Dinnae you do that already?*" Powerful gusts raked the mountainside. Perched on a cliff edge, Rannock turned into the wind. The ferocious updraft buffeted his wings, making the bronze webbing ripple.

"*Aye, but I was asking different questions.*" Frost

crackled, ghosting through the link as Levin wing-flapped, taking flight. *"Gonna need Ivy, Ty."*

"Not a problem," Tydrin said, on board with his mate's involvement. A talented computer hacker, Ivy practically lived in the Hub, computer central inside the Scottish lair. Her skill set was a handy one, upping his pack's influence on the international stage, making it possible to communicate with friendly packs and dig up dirt on rival ones. *"She'll be all over that shite."*

"Good," Levin said, wind whistling through the connection. *"Gonna ask her tae mine the dark net."*

Tydrin huffed. *"She'll love you forever."*

Levin chuckled.

"No fair, man," Tempel grumbled, resurrecting the familiar complaint. *"You're already her favorite."*

"Can we get back to the point?" Kruger snapped, temper threatening to boil over.

Not surprising.

A venomous dragon, his friend landed on the insane side of vicious. Born of a high energy female, Kruger's magic was majestic. Wholly toxic. One hundred percent lethal. Toss in the fact he possessed a long memory, held nasty grudges, refusing to forgive the smallest slight, and "vindictive" spun into "seek-and-destroy." An excellent combination, tremendously useful in a longstanding feud.

Reading his friend, Rannock gave him the outlet he needed to stay even. *"Tell it like it is, Ruger."*

"I want the Danes dead... nothing but piles of ash," Kruger said, the slither and hiss of venom in his voice. *"But if the Archguard's involved, I want a shot at those arseholes, tae. I donnae care if I haft'a go all the way tae Prague and rip Rodin's head off myself."*

The Scottish pack murmured in agreement.

Cyprus shut it down. *"Home, lads. Nothing more tae be gained out here tonight."*

With a snarl, Rannock vaulted off the cliff side. His long metal claws disengaged. Ripped from the sheer rockface, huge stones took a nosedive toward the bottom of the chasm. Watching the carnage, he somersaulted into a sideways flip. Scales flashing in the moonlight, he torqued into a tight spiral and, enjoying the rush, opened his wings. A blast of frigid air caught the undersides, stretching the webbing.

Taut muscles squawked.

Pain rippled over his shoulders.

His headache disappeared, bathing him in relief.

Rannock grinned, embracing the strain, feeling the burn, enlivened for the first time in hours. Buffeted by bitter winds, he banked around a serrated peak and turned east. The city of Aberdeen lay less than twenty minutes away. Nothing but a fast flight home—to the Dragon's Horn, the pub and distillery he owned with his brothers-in-arms. And five stories underneath it, the underground lair he shared with the only family he'd ever known. Good males. Gorgeous setup. Rewarding work. All set within a granite city on the coast of one of the most interesting places on earth.

Beautiful Scotia.

His home.

Nowhere else he'd rather be. Except...

The whisper of her voice came to him again.

Rocketing around the last peak on the eastern lip of the Cairngorms, Rannock rolled in beside Kruger. He flicked his tail. Bronze spikes met emerald-green scales as he bumped his friend. A love tap. The equivalent of "*You good*?"

Bright scales flashing, his friend tipped his horned head.

Rannock bared a fang in response.

Back to even-tempered, Kruger smiled. *"Gonna* not *call her again?"*

"Screw off."

"Haven't managed it yet, have you?"

"Seriously, lad. Screw the hell—"

"Why're you fighting it?" Kruger asked, clear confusion in his pale yellow-green eyes. *"You want her. She keeps picking up the phone, so it's clear she wants you tae. Mon up, laddie. Ask Cyprus for the jet. You could be on her doorstep in less than eight hours. Take her tae bed. Claim her proper. Bring her home. Easy as that."*

"Not gonna happen."

"Why?"

"You know why."

"That's bullshite, Ran, and what's worse, you know it. What happened wasn't your fault. It wasn't—"

"Butt out, Ruger." The headache circled back around, making another appearance. His eyebrow twitched as Rannock threw his friend an aggrieved look. *"Leave it alone."*

Kruger muttered something.

Rannock didn't bother to ask for clarification. Ignoring his packmate, he increased his wing speed and, blasting out of the mountains into thick woodlands, left Kruger to play catch-up. Heavy snow swirled as nasty weather kicked up, mirroring his mood, making him wonder if Kruger was right or... if Rannock just wanted him to be.

Probably.

He couldn't deny he wanted her. Question was... did he deserve her?

A resounding *no* echoed inside his head.

Of course he didn't deserve her. She was light and grace. All things bright and beautiful. Smart, brave, and wily, with just the right amount of attitude. A female with a bright future that would be dimmed by the likes of him. Which meant he needed to stop calling her, then figure out a way to avoid her when she visited Aberdeen. Cutting her loose would be the kindest thing for him to do, but as the glitter of city lights came into view, Rannock knew he wasn't going to change his number.

Not tonight.

One more call. Another chance to hear her gorgeous voice and admire her clever mind. Hours he'd use to get his fix—take one last hit, then file it away with all his other memories of her—before he turned away from the beauty he longed to claim, but never would.

3

T-minus one day

Cate liked the first day of the week best of all. No one ever darkened the door of Kane's Classic Car Restoration on Sundays. The phone never rang. She loved it when the shop closed and everyone went home for the weekend. Prime time for her. Nothing beat being alone without distractions. Or the long stretches of silence inside a garage usually full of mechanics.

The smell of grease and exhaust fumes in the air didn't hurt her good mood either. But even better—the absolute best—was listening to the rumble of a 1957 Chevrolet Corvette turning over for the first time in more than half a century.

Heaven for a girl who craved quiet, but rarely found any.

Sitting in the main garage with a single bay door open, she pressed the sole of her high-top sneaker against the gas pedal. Not a lot. Just a nudge, enough to make the engine rev and her senses sing. Listening for any ticks, Cate gave her latest rebuild a little more juice. The powerful V-8 growled. High-gloss paint gleamed beneath bright overhead lights as the hood shimmied. Keeping an eye on the dash, she gave the Vette more gas, monitoring the RPMs.

Satisfaction hummed through her.

Perfect pitch. Just right. Not a fault to be found in the engine she'd spent weeks rebuilding. Resurrection in the best way for the Corvette. Vindication for her, considering the car's condition when she first laid eyes on it... and the way her coworkers scoffed when she rolled the rusted-out metal corpse into the garage over a month ago.

Too damaged. Bitten off more than you can chew. Ready for the scrap yard.

She'd heard it all before she began to restore a car everyone wrote off on sight. Neglected, forgotten, the classic ride was a throwback to an era many considered dead and gone.

Much like the building she sat inside now.

After powering down the engine, Cate took the key out of the ignition and exited the low-slung cab. As she cleared the frame and shut the door, she looked around the renovated warehouse doubling as Kane's new location.

Old-world charm disguised a state-of-the-art operation. New equipment, computers, and tools. Smooth, unstained concrete floors. Two kitted-out design suites upstairs, with offices to match. Pitted red-brick walls with faded paint that read *Reader's Goods*. Her absolute favorite, though, were the tall, arched, refurbished hundred-year-old windows overlooking the Savannah River. A mix of ancient and modern, a nice find turned beautiful location on the tail end of River Street. Less than fifteen minutes' walk from the hustle and bustle of Old Town Savannah, with its gorgeous squares and old-growth live oaks.

Pretty fancy digs for a garage. One her boss had flipped the *Open* sign on six months ago.

He said he'd done it to keep her happy. She maintained the new place was more for him than for her. Kane liked the high-rollers she attracted with her rebuilds and restorations. Bigwigs with lots of cash preferred visiting deluxe installations. And happy clients made good repeat customers.

Case in point?

The classic Corvette she'd come in to put the final touches on before the buyer picked it up Monday morning. Painted classic red with a white V-slash on the side, the Vette was the third car she'd restored for the same guy. He kept coming back, filling his garage with her custom rebuilds, singing her praises to whoever wanted to listen. It had taken time—years of work—but her reputation as one of the best in the business could no longer be denied.

Hollywood executives had started to call. Fortune 500 CEOs wanted spots on her calendar. Car buffs from all over the States reached out on a regular basis to consult, picking her brain, wanting to talk about making the classic cars they loved whole again.

Kane wasn't complaining.

Neither was she.

Business was good, and given the percentage she now made on each job, her bank account was moving toward healthy. A lucky break. One she credited to her boss.

Most guys wouldn't have given her the time of day when she showed up looking for a job. Kane had taken a different approach, insisting she back up her claims with action, asking her to switch out the transmission in his '68 Mustang GT. After which he'd hired her on the spot. No more questions asked.

A month later, he'd done something else unexpected. The instant he understood what she could do, he'd made the shift, giving her a raise along with profit-sharing potential. Making room in the shop for her rebuilds. Expanding into a swanky location when the bottom line said the move made financial sense.

Nice boost to her ego.

A definite winner in her books, even if it meant more pressure.

Her stomach tightened at the thought. Combating the stress, she blew out a breath and glanced around the shop again. Call her allergic to change, but... sometimes she missed the old shop. The stained floors and dented standing toolboxes never bothered her. And having to MacGyver electrical components for the engine block lift assembly? An added bonus.

She'd enjoyed the fact the thing never worked right, forcing her to get creative with interesting solutions in the face of tight deadlines. Usually under the black cloud of impending doom of a client's arrival to pick up a custom ride that wasn't quite ready.

Spotting a smudge on the Vette, Cate snagged the clean rag from the back pocket of her jeans. With an eye for detail, she ran the soft cotton along the door edge, then over the handle. Fingerprints on glossy red paint disappeared. Her disquiet did not.

So much had changed in the past couple of months. Lots of adjustments. Too many things to worry about. She'd moved into the new shop. Her sister had moved halfway around the world—to Scotland, of all places. And her irresponsible con man of a father had vanished. Again. For...

Cate frowned. Hell. She didn't know.

Her dad ghosted so often, she'd lost track over the years. His reasons changed depending on the situation. Sometimes he left after she and Nicole got on his case about his behavior, and all the people he stiffed. Sometimes he lay low after losing to the wrong people in an underground poker game. Sometimes, though, it was worse.

Life-threatening *worse*.

Her head started to ache.

Rubbing her temples, Cate tried to stave off the headache that always arrived when she thought about her dad's misdeeds. Don't get her wrong, she loved him. A lot. Probably way too much, given her childhood and all the crap he pulled. Her sister rolled with the punches, shrugging off the bad, remembering the good.

Cate found she couldn't be so *laissez faire*. Not after years of being moved from one place to another—all the frenzied packing and midnight escapes out bathroom windows as her father scrambled to avoid whatever mark he'd finished conning.

This time, though, she had a feeling he'd gone too far. Gotten in over his head. Borrowed too much from his bookie. Pissed off the wrong person, someone too powerful to outrun.

The radio silence over the last three weeks directed the assumption. Her dad might be a skilled thief, but he'd never abandoned his daughters so completely. He always managed to get in touch when he dipped beneath the radar. Usually he called, leaving a message on her voicemail. Sometimes he pushed notes under her apartment door or left them in her mailbox. Whatever. The method of communication didn't matter. The fact she hadn't heard word one in weeks didn't bode well, making her wonder if fate had finally caught up with him.

With a sigh, she started toward the bay door. Time

to close up shop and visit another of her father's favorite haunts. She'd checked all the usual places. Made the usual calls. Talked to the usual suspects, then moved on to people no sane girl wanted to meet in daylight, never mind the dark of night. So far, none of her inquiries had borne fruit. A problem, given her flight to Scotland left tomorrow night.

First stop—London, England. From there, she planned to hop a train north. Nicole would meet her in Edinburgh and drive her to Aberdeen. The Granite City. Her sister's new home with a man Cate had never met, but each video chat only made her like him more. He was cool. He was smart, gorgeous, and so in love with her sister it filled Cate's heart with happiness.

Vyroth was the real deal, treating her sister like the most precious thing on earth, and honestly? That was all Cate cared about—that Nicole was happy and healthy. Her sister had gambled big and won bigger, brightening her future, making her dreams come true with a guy who believed she hung the sun in his sky.

All right, so it wasn't perfect. Scotland was too far away for her liking, but... screw the distance. That was what vacation time and transatlantic flights were for.

Her trip was set. The tickets bought. Her bags packed. Everything planned. The only impediment to a happy reunion with her sister? Their wayward father.

"Goddamn it, Dad," she muttered, stepping over a dented bumper on the floor, trying to ignore the knot in her stomach. "Where are you?"

The question caused worst-case scenarios to stream into her head.

Halfway across the garage, fear for him pumped her brakes. She stopped before she reached the control panel that closed the wide steel door. Feet planted in a patch of sunlight flooding the garage, she stared out into the street. Questions poked at her. Was it too late? Was her dad already dead? Had he been buried in a shallow grave... or fed to alligators in one of the swamps surrounding Savannah?

The thought sent her into a tailspin as she watched a dark sedan roll up. Expensive ride. A newer model with blacked-out windows and no brand badges. The sight tweaked her antenna. Could be a Mercedes. Might be an Infiniti. She couldn't say for sure from a distance, but after years of being forced to run with her father, she owned great instincts. Something about the car didn't sit right with her. Overactive imagination, maybe. Paranoia, for sure, but...

Cate never forgot a car.

She'd seen the one idling across the street before —trailing behind her as she left work, parked outside her apartment complex, sitting curbside yesterday evening as she closed up shop.

Forcing her feet to move, acting casual, she crossed to the control panel. Closing the door and setting the alarm system just jumped to the top of her to-do list. She pressed the green button. Gears ground into motion. Heavy-duty rubber wheels squeaked against metal tracks. The door started its slow descent toward the concrete floor.

The sedan's driver door swung open.

Built like a linebacker, a man in a dark grey suit stepped out from behind the wheel. Swanky kit. Suave appearance. Handsome face, pale eyes pointed in her direction. Her nerves jangled as a blond guy, light to the driver's dark, followed the leader, planting shiny dress shoes on cracked asphalt.

Car doors slammed closed.

The pair shifted toward the shop.

Dropping all pretense, Cate tensed as she watched her uninvited guests cross the street. No question about their destination—her and the garage she stood inside. Willing the door to roll down faster, she backed away from the entrance. Halfway down, the door blocked her view, but she heard the clip of well-heeled shoes rapping across the driveway. Dread spiked through her. Her heart started to tango, dancing inside her chest as her fight-or-flight response hit, jetting through her veins.

Swallowing the bad taste in her mouth, she pulled her cell phone out of her back pocket, but... who should she call? Nine-one-one would be the smartest choice, but what complaint could she register? She could almost hear the conversation now.

Operator: Nine-one-one, what's your emergency?

Her: Well, nothing much, really. Just a bad feeling.

Operator: There's no emergency?

Her: Yes and no. Two well-dressed male supermodels are approaching my place of business. They're beautiful, but seem dangerous, and since my dad pisses off scary people on regular basis, I'm thinking—

Operator: Ma'am.

Yeah. Right. Like any of that would go over well.

Something told her telling the emergency operator potential patrons approached her front door wouldn't rate a drive by any black-and-whites in the area.

Tapping her phone, Cate stared at the home screen. A family photo. One of the only ones she had of her and Nicole (ages six and seven) with their dad. Staring at her father's face, she wished he'd been better that playing it straight. Wished he'd chosen a different life. Wished he'd stop dragging her into his messes. But wishing didn't mean squat when faced with a couple of *maybe* bad guys wearing expensive suits.

Chewing on her bottom lip, she kept her eyes on the bay door, backed toward the stairs to the upper floor, and touched her phone app. She scrolled to down to the only person she trusted to answer and hit go. The Samsung went to work. She heard it ring, then—

"*Bellmia*," a deep voice growled. "You done packing?"

Sleepy timbre. Thick Scottish accent.

Her lifeline the last few of weeks. Her calm in the midst of the storm.

Relief whirled through her.

Backing away from the still-descending door, Cate skirted a workbench and whispered, "Ran."

"What's wrong?" A rustle came through the line. A creak sounded, followed by a heavy thump. Sounded like bedsprings then feet hitting the floor. "What's going on?"

"I don't know yet, but if something happens to me... if you don't hear from me, if I don't get on the plane—"

"What the fuck?"

"Ran, my dad's in trouble." Swiping a heavy wrench off the table, she watched a big hand reach under the door. Sensors detected the breech. Breath stalled inside her chest as downward momentum stalled. Rubber wheels reversed course, moving up, pulling the garage door away from the floor. Spinning toward the rear emergency exit, she searched for a spot to hide. Nary an obvious one in sight. The open plan and slick design didn't allow for hidey-holes. "I've been looking for him. Asking questions. Now, there are guys here."

"How many?"

"Two."

"Description, Catie. Now."

She rattled off the details, giving as many as she could. The squeaking stopped. Long shadows entered the garage as the duo stepped inside. "This is not good. Not good. So not good."

"Rear exit?"

"Yes, but it empties onto an alley with a dead end."

Rannock snarled, sounding more animal than human. "Fuck."

Excellent summary. Perfect enunciation. She couldn't have expressed it better herself.

"Run, lass—hide. Call the police. Get to—"

The emergency exit door slammed open. Hinges shrieked, cutting off Rannock's instructions. Reinforced steel hammered the wall, making chunks of red brick fly toward the ceiling. Bigger than the other two, a third man stepped out of the alley into the garage, trapping her between the front door and the back of the shop.

Her brain took a snapshot as she lunged toward the stairs leading up the second floor. Dark hair. Dressed in jeans and an expensive long-sleeved sweater. Nasty expression on his face. Obviously related to the other two guys already inside.

"Shit."

"Cate? Talk to me. Tell me what's happening."

Phone pressed to her ear, she locked eyes with the bad guy. "Three of them, Ran. They're inside the shop."

"Listen tae me," Rannock said, voice even, but she heard the underlying fury in his tone. "They're going tae take you. Don't fight, lass. Stay alive. I'm coming for you, Catie-mine. I'm coming. I'll find you. Just stay alive for me. *Stay alive.* Do you hear me?"

Terror gripped her. "Ran."

"What'd I say?"

Her feet landed on the bottom tread. Pumping her legs, she sprinted toward the top of the stairs. "Don't fight. Stay alive."

"Good, *Bellmia*," Rannock said, voice low, so deep and dark it grounded her. "I'm coming for you. I'm—"

A hand grabbed the back of her jacket.

Cate screamed as a man hauled her backward. She slipped on the stairs. Unable to do as Rannock asked and cry defeat, she raised the wrench and, fighting his grip, swung wild. She aimed for his head. Metal cracked against his cheekbone.

His head jerked to the side, but he didn't let go.

In what felt like slow motion, he turned back her way. Glowing green eyes collided with hers. Terror bumped into shock. She drew in a choked breath.

With a hiss, he yanked again.

Her feet left solid ground. She went airborne. He released her in midair. She landed back-first on the concrete floor. Air puffed from her lungs, emptying her chest. Pain clawed through her. The phone spun out of her hand, hit concrete, then slid across the smooth surface.

Curled on her side, gasping for breath, Cate reached for it. She wheezed Rannock's name.

Full of fury, a snarl echoed through the line in answer.

"Jesus, Dillinger," one of the bad guys said. "Go gently. We need her alive."

"Fuck that. She hit me."

"Get used to it," the third guy murmured,

sounding calm, like a mass murderer in the midst of a bloodbath. "Not as though she's going to cooperate."

"She should."

"Would you?"

Dillinger grunted, then flipped her over. She kicked out with her foot. He knocked her boot aside, swatting away her attempt to nail him, and drew something from his back pocket. Plastic black body. Metal prongs. He aimed the taser in her direction.

"No!" Struggling to evade him, Cate slid backward across the floor. "Stop! Get away!"

"Settle down. It'll only hurt for a second."

He grabbed her ankle and dragged her forward. She heard the awful crackle of electricity a second before metal prongs touched the side of her neck, making her body convulse and her world go dark.

4

T-minus thirteen hours

Fear for Cate at full throttle, Rannock snarled at his bedroom door. Magic rose on a wild hum. Carved from a single piece of hardwood, the door flipped open. Wood slammed against floor-to-ceiling wainscoting. The collection of medieval weaponry mounted to the wall quivered. One of the double-bladed war axes he favored hit the floor with a clang.

Rannock didn't bother to look.

He was too busy moving, storming into the hallway, his mind turning over the facts. Three men. Inside the garage. Invading a place Cate felt safe. Bare feet moving over hardwood floor, he swung into the main corridor. Rannock bared his teeth on a growl. He would kill the bastards for that alone. For entering the space she created inside every day—felt the most comfortable—and tearing away the illusion of safety.

The fear in Cate's voice echoed inside his head.

His pace stalled halfway down the corridor.

The bastards. He'd rip their faces off when he found them.

Heart beating double time, naked as the day he'd come into the world, Rannock conjured his clothes. His brothers would no doubt thank him. Being clothed while he yanked each one out of bed would no doubt win him big points. Maybe enough to grant him use of the pack's private jet so he could fly halfway around the world to rescue a female he'd never met, but needed to keep safe.

Sounded crazy.

His dragon half didn't care.

Whipped into a frenzy by the fear in Cate's voice, his beast wanted out of the lair. Now. No negotiation. Forget about daylight and deadly UV rays. Only one thing mattered—reaching Cate as soon as possible.

Her name echoed inside his head.

Anger burned through him.

His control slipped. Magic escaped its leash, slicing down the corridor. The light globes above his head shivered in reaction. His body did the same, powering up so fast magnetic force spun the metal alloy with tornadolike force through his veins. Door hinges along the corridor rattled. Brass knobs shook as he strode past each room, one thing on his mind.

Cate.

Goddess help him. She'd sounded so bloody scared.

Upping his pace, Rannock rounded the corner into the common room. A comfortable space, one the Scottish pack gathered inside each morning to debrief after a long night of patrolling. The circular room capped by a stained-glass dome usually soothed him whenever he entered. Lots of room to move. Old-world charm. Full of well-worn couches and chairs that invited a male to sit down, put his feet up, and stay awhile.

The huge TV mounted to the wall opposite the stairs leading up to the pub, however, was a recent addition. One Tempel, the newest member of the Scottish pack, insisted he needed to watch the NFL on weekends.

Right now, though, the luxury didn't register. Only one thing did—his mission. Simple Straight-forward. Nothing complicated about it—drag his brothers out of bed, formulate a solid plan, and get airborne.

Not that he didn't already know how he'd handle the situation.

Trained in combat, the mission strategy coalesced inside his head the instant Cate explained the threat. Rannock flexed his hands. Her stupid sire. The male needed his head examined. No father worthy of holding the title put his offspring at risk. Cate and Nicole's sire, however, hadn't gotten the memo. Or maybe he was simply too selfish to care. Either way, the task now fell to him, and regardless of the opposition, Rannock refused to let her down.

Not now.

Not ever.

He'd given her his word. No way in hell would he break it.

Which meant he must line up the details before his departure—and get his commander to agree.

The private jet Cyprus kept on standby needed to be readied. The Hog (the Sea King helicopter Rannock had stolen from a decommissioned army base in the former Soviet Union) needed to be fueled. Precautions must be taken to ensure he arrived at the private airstrip seventy-five miles north of Aberdeen in one piece.

Rannock ground his molars together.

So inconvenient. Shifting into dragon form to

reach the hangar would be faster. More efficient. A better choice all the way around, but he couldn't unleash his dragon half right now. Not with the sun already high in the sky. Rage-inducing, but travelling in daylight was never a good idea. Not for Dragonkind.

Warriors who didn't find shelter before sunrise suffered horrible injuries. Powerful UV rays were dragon killers, stealing a male's magic, dismantling him scale by scale as sunlight acted like razorblades and sliced him apart. The limitation of his kind was one of the many reasons he'd stolen and rebuilt the Hog, not only making it airworthy, but also impervious to the sunlight, allowing his pack to travel long distances during the day. Unconventional, sure, but...

Screw convention.

No way could he wait for nightfall. He needed to leave now. The quicker he got the jet airborne, the faster he'd land and locate the bastards who'd taken Cate. A deep sense of loss moved through him. Longing arrived next, gripping his heart, messing with his head as he skirted one of the coffee tables. Strange. He'd never reacted to a female the way he did Cate. She fascinated him. She amused him. She made him ache with a need so profound he burned with it.

None of which made sense.

Sure, he talked to her on the phone every day. But talking to someone shouldn't lead to *this*—the terrible, messy tangle inside his head. Bloody hell, he didn't even know what she looked like. Not that she hadn't tried to get him on screen in the beginning (after he'd answered the phone by mistake, then lost his mind and kept calling her). Every time she sent a video-chat link, though, he refused to click on it. Seeing her face-to-face would undo him.

He knew it deep down where instinct lived and

self-preservation visited upon occasion. The beast inside him made that clear enough. His dragon wasn't confused about Cate. He wanted her. Craved her. Lived to hear the sound of her voice every morning. Longed to hear it at the end of each day too.

Bare feet brushing over oriental rugs, Rannock vaulted over the back of the couch. As he landed, he shoved an armchair out of his way. The thing tipped over, slamming into the floor as he sped past the kitchen into the corridor on the other side.

He snarled at the doors lining the hallway. Ten total. All closed. No one awake. Zero reaction to the powerful magic frothing around him and into the air.

Clenching his teeth, he fired up mind-speak. Neutrons sparked. The connection solidified. His temper snapped. He roared at his commander, *"Cyprus!"*

Pushed through the link, his voice detonated in the quiet. The mental blast exploded against his temples, then into his brothers-in-arms' heads, yanking each out of la-la land.

Various versions of "*what the fuck*?" echoed through mind-speak.

"Shite. She's in trouble," Kruger said, recovering first. Not surprising. Quick on the uptake, Kruger ate brilliant for breakfast, puzzling things out faster than any male Rannock knew. *"How bad is it?"*

A round of "who" hit the airwaves.

"Cate," Kruger said.

"*Niki's sister?*" Tydrin asked, sounding half-asleep. *"How does Ran know her?"*

Kruger grunted. *"Seriously?"*

"What?" Tydrin grumbled.

"Swear tae Christ," Kruger said with a sigh. *"It's like you donnae pay attention on purpose. He's been talking tae her on the phone for nearly a month."*

"Jesus," Wallaig muttered.

"Hell," Vyroth said, resignation in his tone.

"Totally missed that one," Levin murmured.

Tempel huffed. *"You're not the only one."*

Cyprus chimed in. *"Ran—answer the question. How bad is it?"*

"Bad." Fighting the urge to rip bedroom doors of their hinges, Rannock planted his feet on the wooden floor. He must stay grounded. Cate needed him focused, not out of control. Cyprus wouldn't give him the green light if he didn't keep his shite together and explain. *"She's been taken. I was on the phone with her when the bastards came. I was... She... Fucking hell, Cy. She was scared. So bloody scared. I can still hear her panic in her voice. It's in my head. I can still..."*

"All right, laddie," Wallaig said. *"Hold yer calm. Let us get mobile."*

Sheets rustled.

Feet began to hit the floor.

Bedroom doors opened and closed with quiet efficiency as his brothers stepped out into the corridor, leaving their mates asleep in bed.

Pale violet eyes met his through the crowd.

"I need tae go," he said, words laced with urgency, expression set in stone as he held his commander's gaze. *"I cannae wait. The bastards took her. I donnae know what bullshite her sire's into, but he's dragged Cate into it. I know the timing sucks with the Danes circling, but I need tae get there and protect her. It's a seven-hour flight. Too fucking long, but I promised. I promised her, Cy, and cannae let her down."*

Cyprus nodded. *"Jet'll be fueled by the time you get tae the airfield."*

Relief hit Rannock like a fist. Gratefulness sank deep, wiping away panic, restoring his calm. The downgrade in alarm sharpened his mind. Strategies began to form with greater clarity—all the *if this* then *he'd do that* scenarios. He might be hours away, but planning ahead—preparing for all possible outcomes —gave him the best chance of pulling Cate out alive.

"I'll make the call. Get Malcolm out of bed and into the hangar." Already on the move, Cyprus strode up the hall toward him. *"Who do you want with you?"*

"Kruger, Tempel, and Levin," Rannock said without hesitation.

He chose Kruger, 'cause well... he was Kruger—smart, lethal, the most adaptable on the fly, as well as the male he spent the most time with, in and outside of the lair. Tempel had been born and raised in America and knew the terrain. And given Levin's aptitude for advanced interrogation techniques and ease with computers, taking the ice dragon along went from borderline to no-brainer.

"The rest of you are mated," Rannock said, gaze bouncing between his packmates. *"Your females need you home. And Vyroth, mon, I know she's your sister-in-law and you want in on the action, but Niki cannae get on the plane. Cate's too important tae her. She'll get in the way and fuck up my plans."*

"Agreed," Vyroth murmured, surprising him. *"If it's as bad as you think, I donnae want my mate anywhere near Savannah... or her bastard da."*

"I'll pack a lunch for your trip, Master Rannock."

The comment came out of nowhere.

Everyone glanced toward the lip of the corridor. All eyes landed on Lapier, the Numbai Vyroth had rescued in Germany, and who had quickly become the Scottish pack's go-to-for-anything guy.

Pivoting to face him, Rannock tipped his chin.

"Thanks, Lapier, but do it fast. The second I've got enough fuel in the Hog, we're airborne."

The Numbai nodded and, with a sharp pivot, disappeared into the common room. His destination no doubt the gourmet kitchen hidden behind a pair of heavy wooden doors. Not wasting a second, Rannock followed, moving through the underground lair with purpose. Ten minutes to fuel the Hog. Twenty-five minutes to the airstrip. Seven hours until he landed on foreign soil and started hunting in a city he didn't know, to rescue a female from thugs he hadn't seen, but planned to rip apart on sight.

5

HISTORIC DISTRICT — SAVANNAH, GEORGIA

T-minus three hours

One-hundred-and-fifty-year-old wooden floors creaked as Rathbone enter his private study under the north side of the Habersham House. A throwback to another era, the boutique hotel he owned with his brothers embraced all things old. Old floors polished to a high shine. Historic red-brick exterior with large, curving balconies. Three stories of wide white trim around wavy paned windows designed to allow cool breezes in, but never got opened anymore. And inside? A glorious mix of antiques and new-world charm. Upscale. Comfortable. Exclusive. The best-run hotel in Savannah.

Everyone said so.

And, of course, the reviews on Yelp! never lied.

With a huff, he crossed the pitch-black room. Twirling the woman's cell phone in one hand, he flicked the fingers of the other. His unspoken command whispered across the study. Candles on the altarpiece flared. Light crept into dark corners as flames rose from blackened wicks, flickering into spindles, adhering to his wishes. Why he bothered was anyone's guess. He didn't need the light. Like all of his kind, he could see in the dark, was more comfortable haunting the shadows than standing in the stark light of day.

Footsteps sounded on the spiral staircase.

The floorboards creaked as his visitor stepped into the hallway. Private floor. No guests allowed on the lowest level of the house, so...

Rounding the antique table doubling as his desk, Rathbone tossed the Samsung onto the leather blotter and shrugged. The Armani suit jacket slipped down his arms. Tossing it over the back of his leather chair, he listened to the heavy thud of footfalls move closer. He loosened his tie and, unbuttoning the top button of his dress shirt, prepared for the violent storm about to roll under the massive archway into his study.

His brother stopped on his threshold. Black eyes full of wrath, blond hair gleaming in the candlelight, Noble glared at him. "I don't believe this shit. Dillinger's out of control."

Rathbone's lips twitched. "He didn't hurt her."

"He—"

"Knocked the wind out of her, but softened her fall with a cushioning spell," he said, pointing out the facts, keeping it real, ensuring Noble didn't rewrite history. Protective by nature, more sensitive than most, Noble disliked hurting women. Normally, Rathbone did too, but desperate times called for different methods. His enemies were cunning and brutal, so he must be too. "Not a single bruise on her."

"He zapped her with a mini-thunderbolt."

"Tit for tat, brother," he said, trying not to grimace. Dillinger *had* been a little rough for his liking. "She hit him with a wrench."

Noble grunted.

The sound signaled surrender, and the end of the argument. Dillinger might lack social graces, but his reaction had been instinctual. Muscle memory more than anything else. You hit one of them, they always struck back.

Yanking his tie from around his throat, he flicked his hand. Black silk landed on the desktop with a hiss. "You have any trouble locking her down?"

Noble shook his head. "She's still out. Probably will be for a while. I put her in the Emerald Room."

Pretty suite at the back of the house.

Impenetrable cloaking spell surrounding it.

Only one way in. No way out... unless he or his brothers permitted it.

A good choice, given the hotel was booked solid. He didn't need his guests stumbling onto his hostage, or figuring out the brothers who owned Habersham House weren't what anyone expected—immortals with one foot in the human world and one firmly planted in their own.

"Where's Dillinger now?"

"Sharpening his knives."

"Good," he murmured, watching Noble move farther into the room.

Air rippled. The temperature dropped, swirling into arctic chill, making candle flames flicker and dance. Dressed in faded jeans and a Def Leppard T-shirt, Noble skirted the back of the couch, then took a hard right, walking away from the ornate wood-paneled walls into the center of the study. His bare feet whispered over expensive Turkish rugs. Quiet expanded as he made the trip, striding beneath burnished copper ceilings to reach his end of the room.

He let the silence stretch. No sense yanking his brother's chain. Noble wasn't shy. If he had a problem with the way Rathbone handled things, he'd make it known. And do it fast.

Expression set in hard lines, Noble stopped walking. He stood on the other side of the desk a second, black gaze drilling into his, then did the usual and unloaded his six-foot-six, two-hundred-and-fifty-pound frame on the armchair across from him.

Leather groaned in protest.

Rathbone eyeballed the antique frame, wondering when it might give out. Any day now, given Noble's size. "The best place for Dillinger to be right now is the armory. It'll calm him down."

"I know. The whole reason I didn't get in his grill about the girl." Stretching out his legs, Noble crossed his feet at the ankles. "You really going to let him question her?"

"Dillinger's not getting anywhere near her."

"Then what?"

"She's bait, Noble. A way to draw her father out."

"I don't like it."

"Neither do I, but that asshole double-crossed us. We can't go where he went. She's the key to smoking him out."

Noble grumbled something under his breath.

He raised a brow. "You got a better way to get the TriHexe back?"

Leaning forward, his brother planted his forearms on the tops of his knees. Fingers laced between his legs, he shook his head. "Shouldn't be this difficult. No way should a human be welcome there."

"I know."

"So kidnapping a girl's the only play we've got?" Black eyes full of unease met his. "Seriously?"

Picking up Biscayne's cell phone, Rathbone stared at the cracked screen. He swiped the pad of his thumb over the damage. Uneven ridges pricked his skin as the Samsung lit up. Rathbone barely noticed. His mind was elsewhere, inside the auto-body shop, replaying the scene inside his head. Recall provided more details, things he'd missed the first time around. He'd picked up on her conversation when he exited the car—the sound of her voice, the panic in her tone, the words she spoke before Dillinger engaged and it all went to shit.

His eyes narrowed.

She'd been talking to a man. Someone powerful. Someone *other*. Someone who might be able to go where Rathbone and his brothers couldn't.

An intriguing idea. Perhaps the solution to his problem.

The guy on the phone valued the girl. The promise he made, the urgency in his voice coming over the line, spoke volumes. The mystery man would want Cate back unharmed... as quickly as possible, no doubt the second he arrived in the city, which gave Rathbone more options. His plan still might work. Maybe a new deal could be struck—Cate's safe return for the TriHexe. Simple exchange. But not with her father.

Noble tipped his chin. "What're you thinking?"

Rathbone didn't answer. He moved his thumb over the Samsung instead. A lock screen with a passcode appeared. He murmured a familiar spell. Biscayne's cell phone unlocked. Easy as pie. No match for the power thrumming through his veins. His mouth curved as he tapped on the phone app, then scrolled to the last number called. Time to see whom Cate had been talking to, and just what the monster he sensed lurking beneath the mystery man's surface could do.

6

SOMEWHERE OVER THE ATLANTIC OCEAN

T-minus fifty-two minutes

Sitting in the cockpit of the private jet, Rannock tried not to think about Cate. About where she was, what was happening to her, or the bastards who'd taken her. Hard to do. His mind kept wandering, taunting him with worst-case scenarios, preparing him for the fact she might already be dead.

Gone before he got the chance the meet her.

Or touch her.

Or claim her, like he suspected he should've done the instant he heard her voice. A month wasted. Days, hours, and minutes never to be reclaimed with his maybe-mate. A female more precious than the breath in his lungs.

The thought tortured him, gouging deep, digging into mental spaces best left undisturbed. Clenching his teeth, he redoubled his efforts. Distraction. He needed a *distraction*, before he lost all sense of himself and his dragon half went insane.

Focusing on the small cockpit, he allowed his gaze to travel. Blackened by a darkening spell, magic rippled across the small windows, pooling against metal frames, protecting him from the sun. Unable to see the sky, Rannock changed tact. His gaze traveled over the instrument panel. He re-checked the gauges, monitoring altitude and wind speed, counting down the minutes until he landed on the Eastern Seaboard of the United States.

He'd never visited North America.

Had never wanted to, either.

But with Cate in danger, and his dragon half rampaging, Rannock ignored his wants in favor of Cate's needs, fighting to stay even as he piloted the plane, flying over the Atlantic for the first time in his life. He hoped the trip was his last, but...

No way of knowing.

No reason to draw a line in the sand just yet.

The door to the cockpit opened and closed behind him. Rannock threw his friend a warning look. "I donnae want tae hear it."

"I donnae fucking care." Sliding into the copilot seat, Kruger treated him to a healthy dose of stink-eye. "You need tae pull your head out of your arse, mon. Get it screwed on straight before you lay eyes on Cate."

He knew what his friend wanted to say. No sense fighting the fact he'd come to the same conclusion about a millisecond after he realized she was in trouble and he wasn't close enough to help. "I've got it straight."

"You sure?" Kruger asked, toying with a button he shouldn't be touching. "'Cause after the mess with Heather, I want tae be sure."

"You keep telling me it wasn't my fault."

"It wasn't," Kruger said, tone softer than he'd ever heard it. Gentle tone. Careful words, as though he understood Rannock's pain, but still refused to allow him to shoulder the blame. "She OD'd, Ran.

Was an addict out of control. No way could you have—"

"I was in and out of her bed for months, Ruger."

"You force her?"

"Nay," he growled, insulted by the question.

"She have fun?"

"Of course, but—"

"You get her into rehab?" Twisting in his seat, Kruger raised a brow. "Twice?"

"Fuck you."

"You broke it off, mon. You told her you were done and stopped seeing her. You didnae kill her." Gaze steady, Kruger reached out and gripped the nape of his neck. "Let it go, Ran. You've mourned her, now move on. With or without you, Heather would've imploded. The outcome would've been the same. Her death doesnae make you unworthy of a female of your own."

"Of Cate, you mean."

"Aye."

"She may not be—"

"Bullshite. She's exactly what you think she is, brother—yours."

Holding his friend's gaze, Rannock struggled to understand. A lot of things, but mostly Heather's decision to take her own life. The ME labelled her passing an accidental overdose. Rannock knew better. He had the voicemail, the one he got too late, saved on the pub's landline to prove it. She'd threatened him, vowing to take her own life if he didn't change his mind and come back. If he didn't submit to her will. An awful situation. One so toxic he knew now he should never have stayed. Not past the first night, never mind the weeks that followed.

He understood that now. A year ago, he hadn't. All

he'd felt was guilt. For not saving her. For failing to get her the help she needed. For not loving her when it was obvious she needed someone to.

"Ran," Kruger said, shaking him a little.

"I hear you, lad. I got it. I just..." Rannock paused when his ass started vibrating. Shifting in his seat, he reached into the back pocket of his jeans. The cell phone he used when talking to Cate buzzed in his hand. He frowned as he saw the screen. The video-call function had been engaged. The caller ID said...

Cate calling.

Kruger frowned. "What the hell?"

"Quiet," Rannock murmured as he accepted the call.

A male with dark hair and pale blue eyes appeared on screen. Powerful energy. Unrestrained magic. A male capable of untold destruction. A throwback to the old ways, when immortals ruled and humans believed. A Dreamweaver whom most of the Fae in Seelie and Unseelie Courts believed no longer existed.

Surprise made Rannock pause. Calculation shoved disbelief out of the way.

Keeping his expression neutral, he tipped his chin. "Shadow Walker."

"Dragon," the male said, mouth curved up at the corners.

"Rannock."

"Rathbone," the male said, completing the introduction. "I believe I have something that belongs to you."

"Aye," he growled. "And I want her back... unharmed."

Rathbone tilted his head. "I'm prepared to talk terms."

Not liking the turn of events, Kruger hissed under his breath.

Rannock ignored his friend in favor of staying focused. "I want tae see her."

"You will... when you get here."

Fear for his female rose hard.

Rannock bared his teeth in warning.

"You've my word Cate is well. Unharmed, simply locked away." Shifting in his leather chair, Rathbone leaned closer to the screen. Pale eyes alight with magical fire, he drilled Rannock with a look, one meant to convey the seriousness of the situation. "You get me what I want, I give you Cate. Win-win, dragon."

"Only if I get tae draw your blood."

The bastard smiled, pretending to be amused. The humor never quite reached his eyes. "One twenty-three Kehoe Street, historic distinct in Savannah. Come to the side entrance. I'll greet you there."

Rathbone's hand flashed across the screen.

The call disconnected.

"Motherfucker!"

"Calm down, Ran. Donnae throw it." Quick as a lightning strike, Kruger snatched the cell phone out of his hand. "We may need it again."

What he needed was to reach Savannah and see Cate. What he needed was to rip Rathbone's head from his body. What he needed was violence, the kind of devastation his dragon half always longed to unleash. Breathing hard, Rannock snarled at the blacked-out windows in the cockpit. Nothing less than a dead Shadow Walker would do.

7

T-minus fifteen minutes

Yanking the silk curtains away from the window, Cate threw up the blinds. The waning warmth of the setting sun hit her, casting shadows across the garden beyond the wavy planes of glass. The side of her brain that enjoyed good design took a snapshot. Lots of roses in bloom. Some peonies, bee balm, and azaleas. Live oaks dripping with Spanish moss. Stone pathways meandering past manicured hedges, deep flower beds, and stone benches. No doubt the private sanctuary of someone with money to burn.

Ignoring the picturesque landscape, she tried the window latch. Nothing doing. The lock refused to budge.

She leaned on the round latch, trying to force it open. Stuck. Locked down tight, just like the other four windows in the bedroom doubling as her prison cell. A room she'd woken up in less than ten minutes ago, warm and snug beneath a comforter someone had had the audacity to tuck around her like she was a beloved guest instead of a hostage. Nothing but a pawn in a messed-up game. One who would be used to force her father out of hiding.

With a curse, Cate spun away from the window. Luxury greeted her in the form of a gorgeous bedroom with amazing wallpaper—dark green and gold, with pink flowers and majestic blue herons. She frowned at it, hating the fact that she loved the design. Vintage decor done well always got her motor running. Which was why she refused to look up. After waking in a bed not her own, inside a room she wanted nothing to do with, the beautiful mural on the ceiling was too much for her to bear.

Any other time, she would've taken a closer look, admired each brush stroke and studied the composition. Right now, all she wanted to do was set it on fire. Along with the fourposter bed and matching antique furniture. Which was, by the way, bolted to the freaking floor.

Nothing else in the room moved either.

The collection of heavy silver candlesticks seemed to be glued to the top of the marble mantelpiece. The solid lamps on the bedside tables appeared to be stuck where they sat. The cast-iron bookends sitting on the dresser, same story. No matter what Cate tried to pry loose, she came away empty-handed.

Gritting her teeth, Cate swallowed a scream of frustration. Given a choice, she would've preferred a dank prison cell to a pretty room. At least then she'd know what she was dealing with. Despite the beauty, something was wrong with the setup. Seriously wrong. Off in ways she couldn't clock. She felt it, though. A weird hum filtered through the space, crawling over her skin, making her senses tingle and the fine hairs on her nape stand on end.

Not that she needed the sensorial telegram. She'd already gotten the message.

She was in trouble. Big trouble. The kind her father found all the time, but she avoided like a trip to the dentist.

Sock feet planted on the area rug, Cate closed her eyes. She inhaled deep, then exhaled slow. She repeated the process. Deep breath in. Hold it to the count of four. Let it back out. Inhale. Exhale. Repeat.

She needed to calm down.

She needed to be able to think.

Panic never helped anyone out of a bad situation. Clear-headedness was the goal. Being able to act, and do it quickly, when an opportunity arrived was key. Her dad might've failed in a myriad of ways, but at least he'd taught her how to think on her feet. To fix problems on the fly. To pivot and find other solutions when things didn't go her way.

A useful skill.

One she must employ now if she hoped to—

A sharp click sounded.

Her gaze snapped toward the door.

A chill crept the length of her spine as the brass knob turned. She glanced toward the fireplace. Carved by a master, the single piece of pale marble surrounded an open mouth, hiding a wide chimney. One she thought she might climb, until she took a closer look. The flue was shut tight, affording her zero chance of escape by way of Santa's favorite exit.

Hinges creaked.

The door started to open.

Backing away from whoever planned to enter the room, she searched for her boots. Maybe she could use one as a weapon. Or maybe she should put the pair on her feet, just in case she got the chance to run.

Spotting her Blundstones under one of the armchairs, she raced on tiptoes toward the fireplace. One eye on the door, she grabbed the pair on the fly and, rounding the chair, set up shop behind it. One boot slid on, then the other.

A tall guy with blond hair pushed the door all the way open. Dark eyes landed on her.

Hands curled around the top of the chair, Cate tensed.

He stared at her for a second, then sighed. "Relax, Cate. No harm will come to you here."

"Bullshit," she said, keeping her gaze trained on him. One false move, and she'd...

Her brows contracted.

She'd what? Brain him with one of the candlesticks glued to the mantel? Grab one of the bookends that refused to come unstuck? She swallowed past the lump in the throat. Weaponless. Cornered. Way out of her depth. God. This was bad. So very, very bad.

Suppressing a shiver, she decided to put her best foot forward. "Who are you?"

"My name's Noble."

"No, I mean... *who* are you? Bookie? Art dealer? The mob—which one, Italian, Russian, Albanian?"

Noble shook his head. "Far worse, I'm afraid."

Worse?

Her brain went blank for a moment. What could be worse than the mob?

Digging her nails into the back of the chair, Cate took a fortifying breath. "Let me go. I've got nothing to do with whatever my dad's got going. I have no part in his—" She paused, wondering how best to put it. "—business."

His mouth curved. "I know, but you're our quickest means to an end."

"What'd he steal from you?"

"It's of no consequence to you."

Her eyes narrowed. "Since I'm here *against my will*, I think I have a right to know."

He shook his head.

Cate suppressed a howl of frustration. "If you won't tell me, then why are you here? No offense, but you're not exactly a scintillating conversationalist."

He chuckled. "I can see why he wants you back."

"Who?"

"Rannock."

Her breath caught at the back of her throat. "Is he here?"

"Close."

"How close?"

"Very close." Half turning toward the door, Noble tilted his head toward the only way in or out of the room. "Need you to come with me, Cate."

"Where?"

He raised a dark blond brow. "You want to see your man?"

Unable to deny the force of her need to see Rannock, she nodded.

"Then follow me," he said, a whisper of warning in his tone. "And Cate?"

"Yeah."

"Behave." Already out in the hallway, Noble glanced over his shoulder. Eyes dark as pitch, and just as unreadable, met hers. "You hit Dillinger again, no telling what'll happen. I may not be able to protect you this time."

Wonderful. Truly fantastic. Dillinger must be an absolute psychopath. A true terror. One Noble would rather not challenge, so...

Guess picking up a weapon on the way to wherever wasn't an option.

At least, not yet.

Something told her Noble would notice. He wouldn't react well to her attacking his back. Even if she got the jump on him, instinct warned she wouldn't win. He was too big. Much too strong. More aware of his surroundings than most. Which left her one option—bide her time, memorize every detail, strike when the odds tilted in her favor. That, and trust Rannock to know what to do and how to pull her out of her father's mess.

8

T-minus five minutes and forty-seven seconds

Dusted by shadows, Rannock stood in the park across the street from Habersham House. Thick trees branches creaked above his head. He paid the welcoming murmur of live oaks no mind. He was too busy scouting his surroundings, becoming accustomed to night scents and sounds. To the feel of a city most Americans considered old, but was new by his standards. "Old" meant something else in Scotland.

Eyes trained on the upscale inn, he studied the mansion his prey called home. Three-story red-brick exterior. Tall windows with wide white trim. Thick cornices painted dark grey butting up against a pitched roofline. Roomy balconies running down the west side. A wide staircase with curving stone railings rising to meet ornate double front doors. Lots of greenery in the yard and leafy trees for cover. Neat. Tidy. More striking in person than the pictures he'd viewed online while in the air.

And trapped somewhere inside? Cate.

His one and only, if Kruger had it right.

Time would tell. The moment he caught sight of her, he'd know. The instant he put his hands on her, energy-fuse would take hold and the bonding would begin, confirming what his dragon half wanted to believe—that Cate belonged to him. That he belonged to her. That she was his mate, a perfect match, the one made and meant for him.

An intriguing idea. For most males, anyway.

He couldn't deny he felt conflicted. His monumental mess-up with Heather had shaken his foundation, making him question everything. Who he was, what he valued, the way he moved through the world, and the lives he touched along the way. Heavy thoughts laced with guilt. Unpleasant ruminations populated by what-ifs and could've-beens. What if he'd caught on quicker? What if he'd acted faster? What if he'd steered clear instead of sleeping with her? Would Heather still be alive... or would she have repeated the same pattern with a human male?

Impossible questions.

No pathway to finding answers.

It was over and done. He needed to stop thinking about it, do what Kruger said and put the awful experience behind him. Problem was... memories kept poking at him, dragging up the pain, leaving him to wonder if he was cut out for connection, the meaningful kind. The kind a female mated to a Dragonkind warrior not only expected, but deserved. If Cate belonged to him, he owed her nothing less than his complete attention and unfailing devotion.

Unease ghosted down his spine.

Rolling his shoulders to break the tension, Rannock gazed skyward, to the place he wanted to be, soaring above the clouds, counting the stars, carefree in the arms of cold winds and open vistas. His eyes went where his body couldn't in the moment, searching for constellations through crooked branches dripping with Spanish moss.

His night vision sparked. Orange shimmer bathed the live oak. Birds nesting in bark-lined hollows blinked at him. Rannock tipped his chin in greeting as damp air rolled in, bringing the scent of night-blooming roses. Water splashed in the fountain behind him, reminding him where he stood... and what he was supposed to be doing.

Nerves flattened into resolve.

Rannock returned his attention to Habersham House.

His eyes narrowed. Fucking Shadow Walker. By taking Cate, Rathbone had forced his hand, dragging a possibility he wanted to keep in the dark out into the light. Now he must acknowledge what he wanted to hide—that the idea of meeting Cate for the first time sent him into a tailspin. Which was the height of stupidity. No way he should be uneasy.

He knew her well. Had talked to her every day for a month. The last thing he should be doing was second-guessing himself... or doubting her welcome. She wanted him as much as he did her. He heard the pleasure in her voice every time he dialed her number and she picked up the phone. The fact she'd called him instead of the police when Rathbone showed up at the shop should be all the proof he required. And yet...

Doubt eroded good sense.

Now, he spun like a top inside his own head, going nine rounds with dread. Which left him cooling his heels outside, fidgeting like a green lad, worrying about her reaction to him when he finally—

A hiss lashed his temples. A link into mind-speak opened.

"What's the hold-up?" Levin asked, scales clicking as he shifted on his perch five miles away. *"Trouble?"*

"Nay. Just getting the lay of the land." Magic humming, Rannock tracked his packmates. The ping boomeranged, allowing him to pinpoint each of his brothers' locations. All in dragon form, all cloaked to keep from scaring the natives. Levin on the south side, Kruger perched on a high rooftop to the west, and Tempel? Rannock's lips twitched. The earth dragon wasn't fooling around. Preferring soil to sky, the male burrowed deep underground, digging channels, setting up shop, mapping the city from subterranean levels. *"Tempel—tell me something good."*

"Nice spot. Savannah's got good energy. Great bones. Lots of old souls."

"Ghosts?" Levin asked, sounding intrigued by the prospect.

Kruger hummed. *"Interesting."*

"Not what I mean," Rannock clenched his teeth. Bloody hell. Seriously? He was about to enter a Shadow Walker's den, not go ghost hunting. *"Back on track, lads. Tempel, give me a grid."*

"Big house. Tons of square footage."

"Aye," he said, scanning the front of the mansion again. *"Tell me something I donnae already know."*

"The house you can see. What's hidden beneath it, you can't," Tempel said, the sound of dragon claws digging through rock came through the connection. *"The bastards have a complex underground. Sprawling. Bigger than the main structure. Two stories of interconnected rooms and corridors."*

Kruger grunted. *"Living quarters."*

"Powerful magic surrounding it," Rannock said, sensing the spell protecting the house. Nothing overt. No visible sign of the enchantment shimmering in the

open air. To be expected. Rathbone seemed like the careful sort. It only made sense he preferred to fly under the radar. All immortals did. Drawing too much human attention never ended well. *"No way I'm getting in undetected."*

Tempel growled. *"Well then, good thing the asshole handed you a gilded invitation."*

"I donnae like it," Kruger muttered, the scrape of claws against steel scratching through mind-speak.

"You and me both, brother," Levin said, objecting to the plan. Again. For what felt like the thousandth time. *"You shouldnae be going in alone."*

Rannock shook his head. *"No choice. No clue what I'm walking into, lads. Best-case scenario, I agree tae Rathbone's demands and walk out with Cate. Worse case—I get trapped in there. Need you bozos on the outside tae pull me out if that happens."*

Levin chuckled. *"Bozos?"*

Kruger cursed under his breath.

Tempel chimed in. *"Got an imprint of the underground complex. Want it?"*

"Light me up," Rannock said, preparing for the magical onslaught.

He waited less than a second.

Tempel hooked in tight, using the open link to relay the information. Pain nicked Rannock's temples. He gritted his teeth, holding the line as the ache moved toward agony. Heat burned through his skull. A map streamed onto his mind. Precise layout. Perfect dimensions. Steady lines. The discomfort downgraded from jagged to smooth. Releasing a pent-up breath, Rannock flipped through mental pages, analyzing the blueprints to Rathbone's home.

His mouth curved. *"All set, lad. Thanks."*

"No worries." The noisy rumble powered down as

Tempel stopped digging. *"In and out, Ran. Don't fuck around in there."*

Kruger grunted. *"Retrieve Cate and get out."*

"If you donnae hear from me in an hour, unleash hell," Rannock said, refocusing on the mansion.

His brothers-in-arms growled in agreement.

Rannock put his feet in gear. Striding from beneath the live oak, he crossed the sidewalk and stepped into the street. The spell protecting Habersham House reacted, detecting his magic, sending up an alarm, informing Rathbone of his proximity. Rannock didn't care. Stealth, quiet recon, no longer mattered. He had what he needed—a map of the underground complex pinned to his mental grid and an invitation to enter.

Two essentials if he hoped to get his female out alive.

9

T-minus two minutes and twenty-one seconds

"Your plan is fucking nuts."

Standing in the vestibule off the side entrance, Rathbone glanced at his brother. Feet planted on antique black-and-white tiles, arms crossed over his chest, Dillinger met his gaze head-on. His expression reinforced his opinion, infecting the enclosed space with his bad mood. Par for the course. The male changed the atmosphere of every room he entered. Happy. Sad. Pissed off and in need of a good fight. If Dillinger felt it, other people got caught up in the ensuing chaos.

Easy enough to read. Difficult as hell to contain.

But after centuries of corralling his brother, Rathbone knew exactly what to do. He raised a brow, challenging the male without saying a word.

Dillinger growled low and deep.

Letting the silence stretch, Rathbone shook his head, refusing to defend his decision. Any other time, he would've gotten in his brother's face and backed him down. Tonight, he let the pissy attitude slide, 'cause...

Dillinger wasn't wrong. Not this time.

Tweaking a dragon's tail was never a good idea. Dragonkind warriors weren't predictable. Violent? Yes. Vindictive? Absolutely. One hundred per cent lethal? Without question. Forgiving when wronged? No way in hell.

Which left him in a bit of a bind.

Given a choice, he never would've involved Cate Biscayne... and by default, the dragon warrior about to bang on his door. Sometimes, however, difficult problems called for creative solutions. He needed the Tri-Hexe back. Immediately. No more nibbling around the edges. Diplomacy wasn't working. Threatening those who lived inside the coven would only cause more problems, ones he wanted to avoid. So... only one thing left to do—use what the Goddess had dropped in his lap. Hold Cate for ransom. Task Rannock with sneaking in and stealing his property back to reacquire his woman.

Not a great plan, given the Dragonkind angle, but some things couldn't be helped. The longer his Triad's piece of the puzzle remained in the wrong hands, the more dangerous the situation became.

"Rathbone."

"I'm aware it's batshit crazy, D, but..." He trailed off as the protection spell vibrated, keeping him apprised of Rannock's proximity.

On the sidewalk.

Sixty-five feet from the house.

Well within striking distance for a dragon.

Fine-tuning his magic, Rathbone tracked his guest, sensing when he paused at the base of the stairs leading up to the hotel's front entrance. Animal magnetism rolled as Rannock tested the shield, pushing magical buttons, looking for weaknesses. When the spell gave nothing away, the dragon in human form strolled toward the side of the house like he had all the time in the world.

Big boots hit the stone walkway.

A rush of magic streamed up the narrow avenue.

Live oaks standing sentry along the path creaked in protest.

Eyes narrowed, he funneled his focus toward the side entrance. Heavy footsteps paused at the top of the stairs, then descended, one beat at a time.

"Fucking crazy," Dillinger grumbled. "Don't want him anywhere near here."

Rathbone threw a sidelong glance at his brother. "You got a better idea?"

Jade-green eyes narrowed on him.

His lips twitched. "That's what I thought."

With a sigh, Dillinger shook his head. "Noble's got the girl. He's set up in the study."

"Good," he murmured, gaze riveted to the wide wooden door. "Keep a sharp eye, D."

His brother snorted.

"I want to see how he reacts to Cate."

"You don't think they're mated?"

"Not yet. Maybe not ever."

Dark brows popped up. "What the fuck, Rath?"

"My guess? He hasn't met her. Not face-to-face, anyway. He knows Cate, sure, has some sort of connection with her, but if she isn't his mate, if his dragon half hasn't accepted her, then—"

"We're screwed."

Ignoring his brother's comment, Rathbone dipped his head and rolled his chin against the top of his chest. Taut muscles protested the stretch. A pinch of pain streamed down his spine as he attacked the tension, trying to get loose, knowing he must remain calm. Showing weakness to a predator always ended badly. Usually with lots of screaming and serious amounts of bloodshed. "Success or failure... everything rests on how much he wants her."

"Big gamble, brother."

"Worth it if it gets us the results we need."

Dillinger grunted.

Rathbone turned his attention back to the side entrance. A wave of powerful magic hit the exterior wall. Glass panes, wavy with age, shivered in thick wooden frames. The gilded doorknob rattled. Refusing to make Rannock wait, he murmured a command. The protection spell surrounding his home unlocked, creating an invisible archway in front of the vestibule. Ancient hinges opened without making a sound. The antique door with ornate trim swung inward.

Rathbone tensed as he got his first look at Rannock. He drew a steadying breath. Good Christ. The dragon warrior was huge, at least six inches taller than him, with wide shoulders and a muscled frame. And at six-foot-three, no one considered Rathbone small.

Cataloging the male's strengths and weakness, he scanned the dragon's magical qualities. A Metallic. Bronze dragon with the ability to manipulate metal and turn his enemies inside out with his exhale. Liquid metal, if he had to guess. Nasty stuff that anyone with a healthy sense of self-preservation stayed well away from. Standing just out of range of the outside lamps, Rannock stared at him from the darkness. An excellent strategy. One designed to test whether Rathbone could see in the dark.

Tipping his chin in acknowledgement, he let his own magic out to play. The dragon warrior tilted his head, reading his energy, getting a better sense of the power Rathbone wielded. A second ticked into two before Rannock stepped into the light, and Rathbone got his first real look at him. Long hair pulled into a short tail at his nape. Orange eyes shimmering with internal fire. Body loose. Focus sharp. Forceful presence. Nearly as bruising as his brother's.

Flexing his fingers, preparing for a fight, his guest's attention jumped from him to Dillinger, then moved back again.

"Rannock," he murmured, watching the male like humans watched venomous snakes. Chancing momentary distraction, Rathbone searched the landing behind his visitor. He raised a brow. "Alone?"

"Nay," he said, deep voice thick with a Scottish brogue.

"Of course." His mouth curved. Dragons always travelled in packs. Which meant his guest had backup. Lots of it. Warriors waiting in the wings capable of unleashing waves of devastation at a moment's notice. No dummy, Rathbone accepted the information with grace. No sense lamenting what he couldn't change. "How much time do I have?"

"An hour."

"Fair enough," he said, liking Rannock despite the tense situation. He seemed solid, with smarts and skills to back it up. Excellent news, given the task he needed the dragon to complete. "Come in. Welcome to my home."

"Where's Cate?"

"Not far. Follow me."

Gaze shimmering with the promise of violence, Rannock dipped his head beneath the doorframe and crossed the threshold. Dillinger made a low sound. The dragon snarled back, baring pointed canines. Rathbone swallowed a snort of amusement. Of equal temperament, his brother and the Scot would've no doubt gotten along under different circumstances. Noble too. And given his immediate liking of the male, friendship might've been possible between Triad and pack… if he hadn't rubbed Rannock the wrong way.

Immortals, no matter the subset, gravitated to one another, forming alliances, helping in times of need, meeting in neutral territory to settle disputes.

Hyperaware of the powerhouse prowling in his wake, Rathbone played with the possibility as he left the wide-mouthed vestibule. Turning into a narrow hallway, he headed for the top of the stairs. Maybe when this was all over, he'd invite the horde waiting to blow his house sky-high in for a meal. The future never promised good fortune. Tempers flared. Trouble started. Wars broke out, so…

Befriending a Dragonkind pack held serious upsides.

Wood paneling smoothed into white walls as he walked beneath a tall archway. Plaster-cast moldings spun him toward the lip of a wide spiral staircase. Pace steady, Rathbone descended into the underground complex beneath Habersham House. Reaching the bottom, he stepped off the stone step into the main corridor. Footfalls softened by a long oriental carpet, he turned left toward his study. Rannock followed, staying on his heels.

Dragon magic crackled through the quiet.

Metal fittings on the light sconces rattled. Electricity flickered. Light bulbs blinked on, then off, reacting to the supercharged current in the air.

With a murmur, Rathbone lit the candles lining the main corridor. Soft illumination spilled, lighting his way through the dark. Not that he needed the runway. His night vision never failed him. But a good host provided certain amenities for his guests. Lighting up dark corners, allowing Rannock to scan distant corners without effort, seemed the very least he could do.

Stopping in front a set of triple archways, Rathbone glanced through the opening into his favorite room. He spent a lot of time in the study. More than his brothers, running his Triad's many businesses, managing the investment fund, ensuring money kept flowing. But as he paused in the hallway, the surge of pride he usually got before entering the room didn't come.

To be expected under the circumstances. Everything rested on the next few minutes.

He'd taken a calculated risk without consulting his brothers. Not something he liked to do, but...

Rathbone clenched his teeth.

No going back now. The time had arrived to see if his gamble would pay off. All he could do now was pray Noble had done as instructed. Cate was the key. His entire plan revolved around her. Nothing about it was complicated. Simple, straightforward, the strategy went something like—set her in the chair by the hearth, light a fire in the grate, highlight her to maximum effect, and...

Wait for the fallout.

Turning at the third arch, Rathbone strode into the room. The familiar scent of oiled wood paneling touched by a hint of cigar smoke greeted him. Warmth from a well-lit fire rolled in. The crackle of flames eating through huge logs reached him. The sight and sound reassured him as his gaze cut to Cate. Curled up in the armchair, she glanced his way. One shoulder propped against the stone mantel, Noble tipped his chin. Rathbone nodded in return, then pivoted to watch Rannock enter the study.

Moving like a predator—slow, steady, senses

sparking as his eyes roamed, searching for danger in shadowed corners—Rannock paused just inside the room. Cate's attention moved from Rathbone to the new addition. Her lips parted. She sucked in a quick breath.

Rannock's gaze shifted to her. He blinked, once, twice, looking as though he'd been struck stupid. "Bloody hell."

Cate's aura flared. Brilliant sunburst. Orange and yellow tinged with metallic bronze strokes radiated. The flash forced Rathbone to look away to protect his eyes.

Rannock held steady, staring as the glow around Cate intensified.

"*Bellmia*," the Scot growled.

"Ran," she whispered, popping out of her chair.

Her feet hit the floor.

Heat blasted across the room.

Boot soles squeaking on polished wood, she started running. Her aura blurred into streaks behind her. Breathing hard, Rannock watched her fly toward him. The stunned look on his face turned to awe. His lips parted on her name as Cate vaulted over the back of the low-slung couch.

Magic sparked in the air.

The space around Rannock began to shimmer.

Moving like an inbound missile, Cate kept running.

Ten feet away. Now five. Then three, and...

Liftoff.

Without slowing, she launched herself at Rannock. He locked his frame as she collided with him. Full frontal. Zero hesitation. All need, no caution.

Grunting upon impact, the male went back on one foot, then steadied and wrapped his arms around her.

Whispering his name, Cate burrowed in tight. The dragon warrior curled his big frame around her much smaller one as she buried her face against his throat. Rannock shuddered as his lips brushed the top of her head.

Combined bio-energy exploded into a kaleidoscope of color. A gust of wind blew through the study. High flames flickered in the grate. Candlelight wavered, fire clinging to blackened wicks as the bonding link sank its claws in deep. Rannock jerked in his woman's embrace. Curling her hands into the back of his jacket, Cate held on harder, pressing deeper, seeking more contact.

Rannock gave it to her, slipping his hand beneath her coat, touching her skin as he set his mouth against her temple. The pair moaned.

Rathbone shifted in discomfort.

He should look away, give the couple the privacy the moment demanded, but the beauty of the connection kept his gaze glued to the dragon warrior and his mate. The intensity shocked him. The meaning behind it woke a desire long dead. A well of yearning opened inside him. Long-held questions streamed through the crack in his emotional foundation. What would it be like to be accepted so completely? For the male he was, not what he owned? How would it feel to claim a woman? The one made and meant for him?

Intriguing questions.

Ones he'd spent centuries ignoring. But as he bore witness to Cate's surrender and Rannock's ready acceptance of his mate, he realized mating a woman must be a spectacular experience. Unlike anything he'd ever felt in over two thousand years of living.

His chest tightened.

Rathbone cleared his throat and, getting his act

together, finally looked away. Gawking at the pair wasn't polite. Neither was standing around while a dragon warrior claimed his mate. And yet, despite his unease, satisfaction rose, pushing into relief as he heard Rannock murmur to Cate.

His plan had worked.

He possessed what he needed—a Dragonkind warrior on the hook, one who would protect his mate at all costs. Right. Wrong. None of it would matter to Rannock now. Not with Cate caught in his Triad's trap.

Lifting his mouth from Cate's temple, Rannock nailed him with shimmering orange eyes. "Privacy."

Rathbone pointed to the triple archway. "Door across the hall."

With a nod, Rannock picked up his mate. As she wrapped her legs around his waist, he pivoted and, striding beneath an archway, exited the study.

The vibration of powerful energy dissipated.

Silence descended.

Reacting to the downgrade, the fire sputtered and hissed before re-establishing a foothold. Flames flickered between half-eaten logs. The warm glow reached back into the room.

Mouth hanging open, Noble blinked. "Jesus."

"What the hell?" Dillinger muttered, staring after the now-absent couple.

Rathbone's mouth curved. "Should I say *I told you so*?"

"Not unless you want me to rip your head off," Dillinger said, voice raw with wonder, making his threat no real threat at all. "Did you see them?"

"Yeah."

"I want some of that."

"Claim a woman, D," Noble said, rolling his shoulders, shrugging off the stunning effect of powerful bonding magic. "Though, with your personality, I'm not sure one'll be crazy enough to accept you."

"Fuck off," Dillinger said, reacting the same way he always did to good-natured teasing... with barely leashed violence.

Noble chuckled.

Ignoring him, Dillinger stared after Rannock and Cate. "How much time do we give 'em?"

Good question.

Rathbone only had an hour before the winged horde outside came calling, so no real time to waste. But after witnessing a dragon claim his mate—and with his plan moving in the right direction—Rathbone decided to be generous. Half an hour should do the trick. Rannock would be much more amenable after spending time in Cate's arms. Which gave him and his brothers the upper hand. Finally. After weeks of failure and frustration, he'd found a solution.

A good one. With an excellent chance of succeeding.

Now, all he needed to do was retain control of Cate and hope Rannock managed to do what his Triad couldn't—enter the Witch's Cauldron to take back and return what belonged to him.

10

Blast-off

Wrapped around a man she'd never met, but knew by heart, Cate held on tight. Holding her secure against his solid frame, Rannock strode away from the three men watching him retreat. No hesitation. Zero worry about pissing off the trio who held all the cards. All his focus centered solely on her.

A stunning realization. One Cate knew she shouldn't know.

Somehow, though, she did with a surety that shocked, even as relief pounded through her. The certainty came from Rannock, not her. She could read him, was tapped in somehow, experiencing his relief, feeling his shock, burning with the same need he felt deep in his bones.

One thought, however, trumped it all.

He was here, and she was safe.

The refrain echoed inside her head, making her curl in tighter. Rannock murmured, soothing her with quiet tones. Pressing her face into his throat, she kept her legs locked around his waist. Her hands flexed in the back of his jacket. Cate took a choppy breath, inhaling him, trying to calm down as he carried her across the hall.

His scent curled through her, bringing warm comfort.

Tears pricked the backs of her eyes. "You came. You came for me."

Cradling her closer, he turned his head. His mouth touched her cheek. A zip of static electricity jumped from him into her, ghosting against her skin, enlivening her senses, making her shift against him.

"Catie-mine."

"Thank you," she whispered, lips brushing his skin. "Thank you, Ran. Thank you for getting here so fast."

"*Bellmia*," he murmured, hands drifting down her back. "Are you all right?"

"I'm in your arms, so yes, but..."

"What?"

"I don't like those guys."

"Rathbone and his brothers arenae so bad. None of the bastards touched you. Could've been bad, lass. They could've damaged you in ways I cannae fix."

"Still..."

Her unfinished protest made him chuckle.

She drew in a full breath. The first one since the jerks grabbed her. "They're dangerous, Ran. I don't know what it is about them, but... something's off. I don't think they're normal."

"By your standards, they arenae, lass."

"You feel it too?"

He nodded.

"So... what now?"

"Wait."

She quieted.

He kept walking, and Cate absorbed the feel of him. Strong arms around her. Hard muscles flexing, long legs working, big hands holding her secure against him. She sighed, relaxing a little more, allowing him to carry her away. And why not? After a month of phone calls, she trusted him. He was the voice she woke to every day. The guy she talked to about problems in the shop, how much she missed her sister and... all the trouble her dad caused.

She'd never held back with Rannock. He was the steadiness in a life that was anything but stable.

And now that she laid eyes on him? Cate released a shaky breath. All she wanted to do was explore, get closer, and learn more about him.

Releasing her stranglehold on his jacket, she stroked over his shoulder and... wow. Just *wow*. He was something. A walking, talking dream with rich brown hair and hazel-orange eyes. So big, bold, and beautiful, she marveled at his size. Though why his height surprised her, she didn't know. His voice communicated a lot—his strength, his confidence, the beauty of the soul buried deep inside the man.

Being in his arms, though, was a revelation.

He was much bigger than she'd expected. Tall. Strong. Built for brutality, even as he handled her with care. Breathing him in, she sent her other hand searching. She needed to know. Wanted to explore. Craved the satisfaction of touching him the way she'd dreamed of over the last month.

Shifting her hips, she perfected their fit. He growled low. A soft sigh escaped as she cupped the nape of his neck. Her nails grazed his skin. His steady strides faltered, slowing as she set her lips against his pulse point.

Allowing instinct to lead, she stroked him with the

tip of her tongue. A quick flick. A soft touch. Gorgeous taste. So beautiful, she sucked lightly, drawing more of him into her mouth.

A low groan escaped him.

Emboldened by the sound, Cate stripped the leather tie from his hair and slid her fingers into the dark, shoulder-length strands. Thick, soft, and wavy, as incredible as the rest of him. Fingers playing, she traced his ears with the pads of her thumbs, then stroked over the sensitive spots behind.

He made a rough sound.

She sighed. "You smell amazing and feel even better."

"Catie," he said, the yearning in his voice tempered by caution.

Intuition sparked, and she knew—just *knew*—he was going to shut her down, deny her what she needed. Try to tell her it was too soon—that he'd left too much unsaid and the secrets he held must be brought into the light, spoken aloud before he took her any further.

No doubt all true.

Cate didn't care.

She'd spent a month fantasizing about him. Talking to him on the phone. Sleeping alone in her bed. Waiting for her trip to Scotland. For the moment she saw him for the first time and her dream became a reality. The one she lived now while wrapped around him, his arms holding her tight, his heat all around her.

Unwilling to go let of the fantasy, she set her mouth against his ear. "It isn't too soon. It's been over a month."

"*Bellmia*—"

"I don't want to wait."

"Got lots more tae say, lass. We should talk first."

And there it was—the reasonableness she dreaded and didn't want.

Scraping his scalp gently with her nails, she pressed a kiss to his pulse point. "After."

He shook his head.

"Later, Ran," she whispered, sliding her cheek along his.

Day-old stubble pricked her.

A shiver of delight stroked her, inside and out. Raising her head, she brushed her mouth over the corner of his. A fierce light in his eyes, he met her gaze. Already burning bright, desire flared into an inferno. She whispered his name. His nostrils flared as he took a fortifying breath. Determined to convince him, she dipped her head and grazed him with her teeth.

His taste came to her.

With a low moan, she rolled her hips against him.

His arms flexed around her. "Fuck, you're gorgeous."

"You think so?"

"Aye."

"Then show me how much," she said, nipping his bottom lip.

"Bloody hell."

"Please, Ran."

"I shouldnae, but—"

"Wrong."

"Have it your way, lass," he growled, the vicious sound making her hum with desire. "I'm going tae take you. Claim what yer offering. Forget where I am while I make you mine."

She hummed.

His hands moved. One slid into her short blond

hair, the other travelled down to cup her ass. Holding her secure, he crossed the hallway. A door opened and closed. Darkness descended for a second before the light came on. Her mind took a snapshot. More beautiful wallpaper. Dark antique vanity with pale marble countertop. Black-and-white vintage floor tile. Perfect. A powder room with more than enough space to spare.

Kissing the base of her throat, Rannock turned the key. A snick sounded, echoing through the quiet as the lock engaged.

Impatient, she squirmed against him.

The corner of his mouth curved up. His eyes met hers, then dropped to her lips. Lips a hairsbreadth from hers, he said, "Kiss me, Cate."

Gladly.

Finally.

Halle-freaking-lujah.

After a month of waiting, she had him in her grasp. No more denial. No more distance. No more wishing and wanting with him too far away to touch. Just delight and heat and the promise of intense pleasure on offer.

Heart beating like a bass drum, Cate did as he asked. She kissed him for the first time, stroking deep, delivering her taste, getting a contact high from his as he gave her what she wanted—pulling the tattered pieces of her together, kissing her with so much heat she lost track of everything but him.

11

He should never have given in, but with Cate's hands on him, Rannock lost control. He felt the slippery slide into dangerous territory the instant her mouth brushed his skin. He wanted her so badly. Had waited a lifetime to meet her. The unfulfilled yearning had been with him so long, he'd lost hope decades ago.

Here, now, with her in her his arms, reality took a back seat as need drove him off the road. He tried to pump the brakes, slow her down, and give himself a chance to decide the best path forward, but...

Angling her head, Cate took the kiss deeper.

His engine fired, roaring into uncharted territory, a place where rules didn't exist and he wasn't in control. Nothing compared to Cate. No other female even came close to the way she made him feel and want and... *burn* to claim her in the way of his kind. His dragon half agreed, all-in to give her what she asked. Fuck the consequences. Throw away his scruples, along with the playbook.

Total insanity.

So completely ill-advised.

No way he should be kissing her back, never mind

undressing her. Too bad his hands had a mind of their own—yanking her jacket off, drawing her sweater and T-shirt up, trailing callused fingers along her soft skin. Cate egged him on, whispering to him, telling him what she needed, lifting her arms over her head. He complied without complaint, leaving her half-naked in his arms.

Standing inside the small room, he tossed her clothing aside. Her hands returned to play through his hair.

His conscience squawked, demanding he slow down. His dragon half balked at the suggestion, forcing him deeper into her embrace. Tangling his tongue with hers, he caressed the small of her back, then moved higher. Soft, fragrant skin. She smelled like crushed strawberries with a hint of lime. Beautiful and fresh. Sweet and tart. Just like the female kissing him blind.

Her aura spiked as he cupped her nape. The Meridian surged, butting up against a connection he'd yet to open. One he shouldn't link in and complete. Not yet. Not until she knew the truth about him and...

Goddess help him.

He needed to do more than slow down. Despite his words to her, he needed to stop... right now.

Hands cupping her arse, Rannock set her down on the countertop. Convenient. Dangerous. Just the right bloody height to love her hard. Already snug between her thighs, pressed tight to her core, he had options. His favorite included stripping her down. Scant separation. A few seconds, and she'd be naked, on display, every inch of her his to touch, tease, and taste.

Her nails scraped over his nape. Her other hand went exploring, dipping beneath his shirt, finding his skin, moving up his bare back and over his shoulder blade.

Rannock shuddered against her. Goddess, she felt good. Beyond amazing. She was passion incarnate, open and ready to take him. A wee siren with an agenda all her own. One full of heat and lust and need. He should've known his mate would react this way. Should've been prepared for the fallout. Energy-fuse—the magical bone between mates—was too powerful to ignore. Once a warrior found his mate, his drive to please her became absolute. No negotiating with it. No chance of ignoring it. A male went from zero to fully committed in an instant.

Exactly what he was doing with Cate right now.

Spending hours on the phone with her over the last month didn't help matters. Knowing her only made him want her more.

He knew her hopes and dreams. Understood what drove her and how she felt about those she loved. The loyalty she showed her sire broadcasted his mate's faithfulness loud and clear. An admirable trait. One Henry Biscayne didn't deserve, and Rannock wanted to claim.

Everything about Cate appealed to him. Her fiery passion. Her desire to help those in need. Her drive to be the best classic car restorer in the world. And now that he'd gotten a look at her? Hell. Her beauty drew him too. Light blond hair cut into a short, messy bob. Modern. Hard-edged. The hairstyle of a female who knew herself well, ignored beauty standards, and went her own way. Dark blue eyes full of intelligence added to the picture. A curvy body with a fullness that pleased him completed it.

A powerhouse with a mind all her own. A high-energy female with direct ties to the Meridian, capable of feeding him from the source of all living things. Vibrating at his frequency, her bio-energy matched his to the decimal point. Perfect pitch. Precise nourishment for his dragon half. No need for him to do a workaround. Cate gave him what he needed without effort.

His conscience prodded him again.

Breathing hard, Rannock broke the kiss.

Fingers tightening in his hair, Cate murmured a protest.

His mouth jumped to her temple. He kissed the tender spot as his hands settled, one at the base of her spine, the other at her nape. Holding her firmly, unable to resist, he took a sip of her bio-energy. She shivered and, unresisting, relaxed into the feeding. A channel opened inside her. A click sounded inside his head.

The taste of her hit him.

Delicious. Abundant. Beyond all experience.

With a groan, Rannock widened the connection. White-hot energy surged through the link. Lost in the beauty of her, he drank deep. Cate held on tighter, blooming beneath his touch. Tears pricked the corners of his eyes. Bloody hell. She was everything. His sun and moon. All the stars in his sky. Her generosity turned him inside out as he nestled in, drawing nourishment from the source, taking what he needed to stay healthy and strong.

Drunk on her, his dragon half settled inside him.

Deep in his arms, Cate whispered his name.

He murmured back, soothing her as gratefulness surged into a tidal wave inside him. Swamped, undone by her, he flexed his hands, unable to believe whom he held. His female. Precious Cate. So bloody beautiful she took his breath away.

He might've denied it for a month, but his beast had known the truth all along. All those quiet conversations... her soft voice in the dark. The strength of her spirit spoke volumes, coming through the line each day. The entire reason he kept calling. No matter how many times he told himself not to call her, the need to know more about her drove him forward. He hadn't been able to get enough.

Now, he understood why.

So full his fingertips tingled, Rannock shut down the connection. Cate sighed. His mouth drifted back to hers. He kissed her softly, thanking her, pleasing her while he took and she gave. Caressing her with gentle strokes, he palmed her ribcage. She shifted in welcome, wanting his touch. Rannock didn't deny her. Tangling his tongue with hers, he cupped her breast. Soft weight in palm, nipple tight. He set the pad of his thumb over the tip. She arched, rolling her hips, riding the ridge of his erection as he applied more pressure.

A bad idea.

He hadn't lied. It was too soon to make love to her. Things needed to be said and information shared to ensure Cate understood the magnitude of accepting his claim. The decision to mate a Dragonkind warrior always rested in the female's hands. She held the all the power. The male owned nothing but blind hope. Which meant...

No more messing around.

He needed to come clean. Be honest. Tell her truth before she went so far, she couldn't go back.

Mating him would change her life. His world would upend hers. Forget about Savannah, Georgia and the garage. Accepting him meant leaving her old life behind. Halfway didn't exist for his race. Dragonkind went in whole hog. All or nothing. High stakes. Big consequences. A tough pill to swallow for anyone. Heartbreaking loss for a female who loved her sire, and had worked hard to build a career she enjoyed in the city she called home.

The realization shook him.

Murmuring in regret, Rannock retreated, breaking the kiss.

"No. Don't."

"*Bellmia—*"

"No talking."

Breathing hard, Rannock grabbed the tail end of his control. He yanked, dragging it out of the void. His beast snarled in frustration. Clinging to resolve, he squeezed her waist and raised his head. Dark blue eyes full of heat met his. Wanting nothing more than to kiss her again, he swallowed and soldiered on.

"Catie-mine, we need tae talk. There are things you need tae know before we go any—"

"I already know, Ran."

"Know what?"

"About Dragonkind."

Surprise lashed him. Rannock froze. "What?"

"Irish twins."

He frowned, not understanding. "Irish twins?"

"Niki and I... we're Irish twins, born eleven months apart." Seeing his confusion, she cupped his face. Tracing the ridge of his cheekbones, she held him in the palms of her hands. "We're close. So close, we share everything with one another. And when I say everything, I mean *everything*."

His jaw dropped.

He stared at her as incomprehension spun him around the lip of the impossible. One second ticked into more before his brain came back online. Shock bled into understanding. Goddess help him. Someone needed to tan Nicole's hide. Either that, or cut off her access to the internet. The fewer videoconference calls Vyroth's mate made, the safer Dragonkind would be.

A low snarl escaped him.

"Relax." Drawing soothing circles on the side of his neck, Cate pulled his attention back to her. "Niki hasn't told anyone else. She won't either. It's just—"

"Irish twins."

"Sisters." Cate shrugged. "It's a thing."

"Undoubtedly." Still surprised Cate possessed knowledge she shouldn't have, he shook his head. Unbelievable. Two females had managed to game the system, doing what no one else in the history of Dragonkind ever had—share classified information across continents without anyone being the wiser. "How much did she tell you?"

Her eyes wide, Cate tilted her head, answering without words.

"Bloody hell," he muttered, realizing everything really did mean *everything*. "Vyroth's going tae lose his shite."

"Love my sister, Ran, but..." She pursed her lips, dragging his attention back to her mouth. "Her dragon, her problem. Right now, I'm more interested in getting to know mine better."

Her comment jolted through him. His chest tightened. Fighting to stay even, Rannock drew a much-needed breath. "You accept me?"

"Yes."

"Truly?"

"Do I look unsure?"

Hunting for the truth, he tapped into her bio-energy. Steady stream, clear intentions, no spike her aura or nervousness in his mate. Nothing but certainty in a female who knew her own mind. The realization freed him. He could take her, make her his without guilt or reservation. Cate wanted him. Really *wanted* him. Not for a night. Not for a quick fuck in a bathroom lined with ridiculous wallpaper. But for a lifetime.

"Fucking hell," he rasped. "You mean it. Just like that, no hesitation at all."

"Babe," she said, unleashing an American endearment.

Any other time, he would've laughed at her audacity. Right now, all he could do was hold on as she leaned forward. Soft lips brushed his. A gentle kiss full of understanding. A touch meant to reassure and soothe—to help him move toward the mental space she already occupied.

Goddamn.

His female... one-hundred percent spectacular.

So strong she humbled him.

Another soft kiss, and Cate leaned away. "I spent the last month with you in my ear, wanting nothing more to be there while being a world away. I know you, Rannock. I trust you. I'm yours, and you're mine. We may only have just met, but I've been certain of that for a while. Now, can we please—"

Rannock didn't let her finish.

Accepting her words as gospel, he dipped his head and invaded her mouth. Heated kisses turned into busy hands. She shoved the jacket from his shoulders and dragged his T-shirt up his back. Her lips left his as she yanked it over his head. Cotton left his skin. Small hands landed on his chest. She exploded, touching him everywhere she could reach. Needing her naked, he lifted her arse off the counter.

A quick snap undid her jeans.

A quicker zip bared her to open air.

His fingers slid beneath denim and... all the way in. Slick, hot, and wet met his fingertips. She jerked in his arms, raising her hips, giving him more access, encouraging him as he played in her heat.

One stroke. Another between her folds, then more.

He broke the kiss to watch her squirm. Amping her up, he buried two fingers deep. Her breath hitched. Showing no mercy, he flicked her clit, circling the tight bud, watching her respond, adjusting the pressure, learning what pleased her. Thighs spread wide, she tipped her head back. He upped the pace and shifted her to end of the vanity. Her arse slid along marble. Working her hard, finding all her sensitive spots, he palmed the side of her throat with his free hand.

Her gaze met his.

"Lie back, Cate."

A needy sound left her throat.

Sinking his fingers deep, he stroked over a place she liked. Twisting, she arched against him. Rannock growled in satisfaction. So close. His mate was so close to coming. With just his fingers inside her. He murmured the instruction again. Cate complied. As her back touched down, she raised her arms and curled her hands around the opposite end of the counter.

"Beautiful, lass."

"Ran."

"Hold on, *Bellmia*. Gonna ride you hard the first time."

Her hips shifted. "Oh yeah."

He grinned, then got to work. In seconds, he stripped her down, flipping her boots off, yanking her jeans down and socks off. Scraping his teeth along the arch of her foot, Rannock paused to admire her. Pretty pink lingerie showcasing her beauty. Pale skin on display. Full lips parted. Heated blue eyes pointed at him.

She made a low sound in the back of her throat.

Ignoring the prompt, he ran his hands over her, tracing her curves before cupping her breasts over the lace.

"Ran," she breathed.

"Christ, you're glorious, lass. A feast just waiting tae be eaten."

She moaned.

He yanked the cups of her bra down. Nipples the same color as her underwear. Gorgeous buds, begging for his attention. Accepting the invitation, he planted one hand on the counter and, leaning in, scraped his cheek along her skin. Day-old stubble grazed her. She gasped. He turned his head and sucked a bud into his mouth. Her head tipped back. Needing more of her, he lashed her with his tongue, then sucked hard.

"Love that, babe."

"More?"

"Yes."

"What do you say?"

"Now. More. Right now, Ran."

Holding her between his teeth, he nipped her gently. "Try again, lass."

"God."

"Not quite," he murmured. "Surrender, Cate. Beg me for the pleasure."

She quivered underneath him.

Pushing the pace, he slid his hand back into her panties. The pad of his fingertip slid over her. He pressed and circled, then stilled. Firm pressure. Zero movement. Her hips rose. Teasing her to get what he wanted, he backed off, leaving her wanting.

She cursed under her breath.

He growled against her breast. "Give me what I want."

"Freaking hell."

"*Bellmia*—"

"Please... *please*, Ran."

"Need me?"

"Please!"

"Beautiful, Cate. Fucking gorgeous."

Giving one last hard suck, Rannock straightened and yanked his button fly open. "I'll taste you properly later," he growled, craving the taste of her core on his tongue but, in the moment, needing to be inside her more. Hooking the silky sides, he dragged the scrap of lace down her legs. "Raise your knees. Spread for me, lass."

Cate obeyed, opening wide, welcoming his possession.

One hand palming her arse, the other curved over the top of her thigh, he positioned and thrust deep. She arched on the marble slab, keening as he took her with one powerful stroke. Buried to the root with her sleek heat gripping him, Rannock closed his eyes. Bloody hell. She was more than glorious. His mate was perfect. So hot and tight she tested his control.

She wrapped her legs around him.

With a growl, Rannock opened his eyes and, taking her in, started to move. Firm strokes. Fast pace. Unfathomable delight. She took him like she'd been born to hold him, lifting her hips, rolling into each thrust, driving him higher as he drove into her. Feeling the clutch of her sex, seeing her breasts sway and her blue eyes fill with pleasure, he rode her hard, sinking deep, sliding out, demanding a response.

Cate didn't disappoint. Enjoying the ride, she begged for the pleasure.

Needing to see her come, Rannock slid his thumb to the top of her sex. Gaze riveted to her face, he caressed her clit, drawing soft circles around her.

She shook her head. "Too much."

"Not nearly enough," he said, stroking her over and over until each of her breaths became moans. "Let go, Cate. I want tae see and feel it."

"Shit," she rasped.

"Go, baby."

Her spine arched.

Mouth open on a silent scream, she throbbed around him.

Baring his teeth, Rannock rode her through her orgasm. Lifting her into each stroke. Watching the pleasure on her face as she gave him his due.

Another flick over her sex.

Cate came again.

Pleasure blasted through him. His balls drew up tight. Rannock snarled as she dragged him toward the edge. Unable to hold on, he let go, coming deep inside her, flooding her with his seed, marking her with his scent, drowning in bliss as he folded forward. Heart hammering, he buried his face in his female's throat, luxuriating in the feel of her as she wrapped him up, enclosing him a warm embrace, making a dream he hadn't believed possible come true.

12

Drowsy with pleasure, Cate came back to herself a little at a time. Quiet drifted. Time stretched. Her synapses fired, falling into each other like playing cards. The mental shuffle ruffled through her.

She cracked her eyes open.

Blurry surroundings came into clearer focus. Mind still drifting, body at attention, she catalogued the physical details. Vintage gold, black, and silver wallpaper. A gilded mirror to her left. Wide crown moldings above her head, under-mount sink and warm marble at her back. Hard body pressed against hers. Strong arms wrapped around her. Muscled hips nestled between her thighs. Warm breath drifting against the side of her throat.

Her mouth curved as delight curled through her.

She sighed.

Rannock in all his glory.

Hands flat against his back, Cate turned her face into his hair and breathed him in. Spicy scent full of musk and man. She closed her eyes. God, he was beautiful, from the top of his head to the tip of his toes. Rough exterior, but gentle with her. A skilled lover. Bossy in bed. Generous when doling out orgasms. Perfect for her. She may not have known she liked a dominant guy between the sheets (or on a countertop), but Rannock's insistence she surrender upped the stakes, heightening her pleasure, making her come harder than she ever had before.

A touch curious. More than a little alarming.

Cate knew herself well. She was a strong woman with modern sensibilities. Confident in her abilities. Determined to succeed on her own. Nowhere near submissive, in or out of bed.

But with Rannock? Biting the inside of her cheek, she replayed the way he made love to her. Assertive. Assured. One-hundred percent in charge and...

She'd liked it.

A lot.

So...

All bets were off. Normal was no longer *normal*. The status quo simply wouldn't do. Not anymore. Not with the dragon she held in her arms.

Dipping her chin, Cate kissed the top of his shoulder. She'd suspected weeks ago she was lucky to have him. Now she knew the truth. Everything about Rannock felt right. Like destiny set on a strong foundation. Like true love bundled up tight in *the one*. Her sister always laughed when she said things like that, but Cate believed in love at first sight. She had her whole life.

Nicole was the skeptic. Cate was the believer. Separate approaches born out of the chaos their father left in his wake.

One daughter questioned everything and trusted few. The other buried her head in the sand, dreamed big dreams, and chose to believe in fairytales. Night and day. Opposite ends of the emotional spectrum. Two different reactions to the same trauma. Both warranted. Both necessary. Both adopted in order to survive an irresponsible father who loved, but had no idea how to raise two little girls.

As thoughts of her dad invaded, the peace of glorious aftermath began to fade. Her muscles twitched. Her mind sharpened, inviting worry back into her mental sphere.

Cate clenched her teeth.

Her freaking father. Good. Bad. One way or another, he always managed to crash the party.

The second she thought it, Cate wanted to take it back. Her dad was missing, and had been for weeks. He could be in hiding, sure, but...

He also might be dead.

And what was she doing? Berating him for ruining her moment with Rannock. And yet, despite the guilt, she clung to the feel-good glow, snuggling into her dragon, holding on tighter, burrowing in deeper, seeking solace in his arms.

Drawing a breath, she reveled in the size and strength of him, along with the comfort he brought her. Another round of thankfulness rushed through her. Overwhelmed, Cate murmured a string of incoherent words. Little nothings. Important somethings, telling him how happy she was he'd found her, how good he felt against her, how much she liked the way he made her feel.

He purred, the sound so full of contentment she smiled.

"*Bellmia*," he murmured, sounding half-asleep.

"Hey," she whispered, drawing her fingertips over his bare back.

"You okay?"

"Never better. You?"

"Feeling a wee bit weak in the knees. You did me in, lass."

"Liar," she said, laughing.

His head came up. The corners of his eyes crinkled a moment before his expression smoothed out. Planting his elbow on the counter, he took some of his weight from her, then threaded his fingers through her hair. He rubbed the strands together, learning the texture, watching his hand play before turning his palm to cup her cheek.

"My mate... So beautiful." He brushed his thumb over her bottom lip, a gentle stroke. Gorgeous sentiment behind it. Her chest went tight. A fierce light in his hazel-orange eyes, he caressed her again. "Thank you, Cate."

Distracted by his touch, she blinked. "For what?"

"Agreeing to be mine."

"Don't do that," she whispered as blinding emotion swept through her, making her eyes sting.

"What?"

"Make me cry after I've just had the most amazing orgasm of my life."

His lips twitched. "Tough chick."

"You know it."

"Well then, hate tae disappoint, but..." He paused to trace the curve of her eyebrow. "It cannae be helped. You need the words as much I need tae give 'em tae you."

"Ran—"

"You're important, Cate. Everything tae me."

Losing the battle, Cate felt tears pool in her eyes. She couldn't stand it. Just couldn't. Rannock was more than *everything* to her. He was her beginning, her end, and every road in between, filling the hollows deep inside her, clearing away the debris of the past to gift her with a brand-new future.

Throat so tight it hurt, Cate took a shaky breath. "You're the beautiful one. You keep saying it's me, but it's you. It's always been you."

"*Bellmia*—"

"I think I fell in love with you day one. The second I heard your voice, I knew I was done. That I was yours and would be forever."

"My beautiful Cate. So brave. So fierce. All mine." Gathering her up, Rannock pushed upright. As he stood, he drew her with him. Setting her on the edge of the counter, standing between her thighs, he framed her face with his big hands. "You love me?"

"Yeah. I know it's fast. Maybe I should've waited to tell you, but—"

"I love you too."

"God," she said, closing her eyes, fighting to keep her tears from falling. "You've gone and ruined me."

"Nothing wrong with crying, lass."

"You cry a lot, tough guy?"

"Once a week... at least."

She huffed in amusement. A tear tipped over her bottom lashes. Holding her gaze, Rannock wiped the wet trail away as she murmured, "Such a terrible liar."

His mouth tipped up at the corners.

Grasping his wrists, she pulled his hands away from her jaw. The second he released her, she burrowed in, pressed her breasts to his chest, her core to the open fly of his jeans, closing her arms and legs around him. With a rumble, he buried his face in her shoulder and hugged her back. Wrapped secure in his embrace, Cate let herself go, allowing herself to *just be*.

Be in the moment with the man holding her. Be inside a bathroom inside a beautiful house, instead of worrying about the problems that existed outside it.

"*Bellmia*?"

"Yeah?"

"We need tae move," Rannock murmured against her skin.

"Do we have to?" Tucked against him, not wanting to be anywhere else, Cate shook her head. "We could stay here. Live here. Maybe someone'll slip us crackers under the door."

Rannock chuckled.

She sighed. "They're getting restless, aren't they?"

"Aye. Rathbone's about tae—"

A knock sounded on the door. Heavy-handed knuckles. Plenty of impatience.

"Time tae get dressed, lass."

A growl wove its way in from the corridor. "Dragon."

Planting a kiss beneath her ear, Rannock lifted his head. "Five minutes, Rathbone."

"Contact your pack," Rathbone said, deep voice rumbling. "Before they blow us all to kingdom come."

Raising a brow, Cate mouthed, *Kingdom come?*

Busy drawing the cups of her bra over her breasts, Rannock shrugged. She let his silence go, knowing she shouldn't find anything about the situation funny. Nothing about being trapped inside a house owned by men she suspected of wielding supernatural powers amounted to a good time. The instant she stepped outside the bathroom, her interlude with Rannock would be over. Reality would rush back and force her to confront a hard truth.

Closing her eyes for a moment, Cate took a deep

breath and resettled her mind. Time to set the fairytale aside and face the issue head-on. What she and Rannock faced—fixing her father's mistake—wasn't going to be pleasant. Nowhere near enjoyable at all.

13

Keeping his mate close, Rannock walked beneath the center archway into the Shadow Walker's study. Beautiful space. A masculine room with floor-to-ceiling wood paneling and old-world charm. The kind of place that invited a male to sit down and put his feet up. Maybe smoke a good cigar. Drink an expensive glass of Scotch. Block out the noise of a busy city and stay awhile.

Relaxed. Roomy. The smell of good coffee and chicory in the air.

A total trap.

One meant to lull him into a false sense of security.

Standing next to a breakfast bar, holding a stainless-steel coffee carafe, Rathbone glanced over his shoulder. "All set?"

"My brothers will hold..." Stopping beside a studded, low-slung leather couch, Rannock drew Cate closer. Her hand flexed in his. He squeezed back, gaze riveted to the other males in the room. Big. Well built. Powerful magic humming just beneath each one's surface—fires banked but burning. Include Rathbone in the mix, and he had a walking, talking triple threat on his hands. "For now."

"Good," Rathbone murmured, grabbing a mug off the tray. Flipping it upright, he poured coffee into glazed pottery. The scent of chicory grew stronger. Dressed in a fancy suit and tie, he pivoted and raised a brow. "Java?"

Cate's stomach growled.

Shoulders planted against the wall by the hearth, the dark-haired male scowled.

The blond holding up the stone mantel with his shoulder chuckled. "Breakfast's on its way, Cate."

"Stop being nice to me, Noble," Cate said, a snap in her voice. "I'm not eating anything you—"

Rannock squeezed her hand, stopping her mid-tirade. "You need tae eat, lass."

"What if they—"

"No one's getting poisoned here," Rathbone said, eyes sparkling with amusement. "We don't kill that way."

"Terrific," Cate mumbled, glaring at the blond.

Green eyes narrowed on her.

Reading the male's expression as a threat, Rannock snarled at him. The male's lip curled in response.

"Play nice, Dillinger." Rathbone moved away from the bar. "Your mate took an instant disliking to my brother."

Cate bristled. "Can you blame me?"

Rathbone shrugged. "Get to know him and—"

"No, thank you," she said, tone prim and proper.

Clenching his teeth, Rannock swallowed the urge to laugh. His mate. Goddess, she impressed him. Even now, while surrounded by the enemy, in the midst of an uncertain situation, she held her ground, refusing to back down, making him so proud he struggled to control his reaction. The beast inside him helped, rising to his surface with such savagery Rannock tensed.

Taut muscles bracketing his spine flickered. Magnetic force slithered beneath his skin. The need to unleash unspeakable violence curled through him.

Feeling the shift in his mood, Cate changed her grip on his hand. Soft skin and smooth calluses grazed his palm as she laced her fingers with his. The comforting gesture burned through him. The urge to rip Rathbone's head off was downgraded from *must do* to *maybe later*. A creature of immediate action, his dragon half protested the delay. Corralling his beast, Rannock drew a calming breath, then turned his attention back to the source of his ire.

His eyes narrowed on Rathbone. "Your terms, Shadow Walker."

Taking a sip from his mug, Rathbone frowned. Steam curled from his cup as he turned back to the breakfast bar, picked up a small pitcher, and added more cream to his coffee. Moving with controlled precision, Rathbone took another sip.

He sighed.

Rannock growled.

The bastard's pale gaze met his. He raised a brow. "Perhaps Cate could step—"

"Nay. My mate stays with me," he said, setting terms of his own.

Though he might be separated from her eventually—depending on the task Rathbone required him to complete. Rannock knew the stakes without having any laid out. Cate's freedom for his compliance. For the retrieval of whatever Henry Biscayne took from Habersham House.

Frowning, he stared at Rathbone. He understood

the game, knew how to play it, but for one problem. He was missing a vital piece of information.

Nothing about the Shadow Walker's strategy made sense. The bastard couldn't have known a Dragonkind warrior was involved with Cate, or that he would protect her at all costs. Which meant Rathbone had planned to take her all along... but for a different reason. One other than to force another magic wielder—a warrior with a strong pack at his back—to do his bidding.

Excellent theory.

Solid argument.

A worrisome thread to follow.

The possible reasons for Cate's abduction were endless. Rannock took a stab at it anyway. Whatever Henry Biscayne had stolen from Habersham House must be of tremendous importance. A matter of life and death for Rathbone and his brothers. No matter how brutal, the trio didn't seem like the types to target innocent females. Fact, not fiction. He read it in each male's bones, saw it in the way each held himself. None of the three liked what they'd done to Cate. Dillinger, with his pissy attitude—and his poorly veiled attempt to hide how he really felt about kidnapping a female—included.

Honorable males. All three.

Under normal circumstances.

Gaze jumping from one Shadow Walker to the next, Rannock put the puzzle together. The last piece clicked into place. He sucked in a quick breath. "Bloody hell. You planned to trade her. Her father took it. You need it back. Whoever has what you want gave you an ultimatum, her for—"

"The TriHexe, yes," Rathbone murmured.

Cate flinched. "What?"

"Steady, lass."

She drew a shaky breath. "But—"

"The plan changed the instant Rathbone realized who I am," Rannock said, focus glued to the trio's leader. "And what my pack and I are capable of doing."

"Right again." Glancing at Cate, Rathbone tipped his chin. "My apologies, Cate. I did everything possible to avoid taking you—working back channels, negotiating with underlings, sending human crews in to steal it back, but all my plans failed. The humans I sent were delivered back to me in pieces. The Blind Witch refuses to negotiate. All she wants is—"

"Me."

Rathbone nodded. "Yes."

"Why? I've never met… I don't even know…" Cate whispered, her voice fading to nothing.

"Your father." Crouching in front of the hearth, Noble added another log to the fire. He tossed in a handful of wood chips on top. Flames hissed. Embers sparked. The smell of wood smoke and cedar spilled into the room as he turned to Cate. "He's become something of an amusement for her. A master thief capable of stealing whatever she wants without her having to leave the protection of her coven. For her, one is good, two is better."

"I'm not a thief. That makes no sense."

Noble shrugged. "Dealing with witches never does."

Rannock growled. "So, my mate for the return of the TriHexe?"

"Precisely." Setting his mug down on a massive desk, Rathbone crossed his arms, then leaned back against the wooden edge. "The place she calls home, we cannot go. The enchantment surrounding the

Witch's Cauldron is designed to trap and bind unwelcome Fae. If we go in, my brothers and I will not come back out."

Lovely story. A little too simple for Rannock's liking. There must be a catch. No way would Rathbone share so openly without a trump card up his sleeve.

"What's tae keep me from walking out with my mate right now?" Rannock asked, testing the boundaries, afraid of what he would find. "With my pack at my back, no way you can stop me."

"The instant she leaves Habersham House, she'll die." Pushing away from the wall, Dillinger flexed his hands. Green eyes flickered in discomfort as he stared at Cate, then looked at Rannock. "Unless one of us removes the pod nestled against the base of her skull."

Alarms went off inside his head.

Shaking free of her hand, Rannock spun to face her. Jolted by the abrupt movement, Cate jerked as he raised his hands. One landed on the side of her throat. The other cupped the back of her head. Holding her secure, he sent his senses searching. Magic hummed through his veins. He funneled the power through his fingertips, hunting for the pod, hoping the bastard lied, praying the claim amounted to nothing but a scare tactic.

He located it on the second pass.

Small. Barely detectable. One hundred percent deadly.

Fueled by unbreakable magic, the seed contained enough explosives to blow his mate's head off. Dillinger was right. The second Cate stepped off the premises, outside the protection spell surrounding Habersham House, she'd die. Instantly. Horribly. No way for him to prevent it.

He flexed his hands in her hair. "Fuck."

Blue eyes wide with fear, Cate swallowed. "They did something while I was unconscious, didn't they? Can you feel it? Is it really inside my head?"

"Aye."

"Can you—"

"Nay, *Bellmia*," he said, stomach churning with dread. "I cannae remove the pod without setting it off. My magic is much different than theirs."

She closed her eyes. "My freaking father."

Fear for her punched through.

Rannock drew her into his arms. Cate snuggled in, seeking his warmth. He gave it without reservation, reassuring her with his touch as he met Rathbone's gaze. "I need details."

"You'll have everything you require," Rathbone said, voice quiet, regret in his eyes before he looked away. "Come back with the TriHexe, Rannock, and I'll remove the pod from your mate's head. She'll suffer no lasting harm."

Rathbone better be right.

Rannock already planned to kill him. But if anything happened to Cate, he'd take his time. Make it painful. Stretch out the torture. Take him back to Scotland and make him bleed for decades. And his word was his bond. No word of a lie.

14

Snug and warm in the middle of the king-size bed, Cate lay curled in the protective cove of Rannock's arms, head on his chest, legs tangled around one of his. Naked, vulnerable, wide awake when she ought to be sleeping. And—according to the placard screwed to the exterior of the wooden door—back inside the Emerald Room. Pretty wallpaper, brass fittings, ornate fireplace and all. Her prison once again, as she listened to the sound of her dragon breathing.

Deep inhales.

Even exhales.

Steady and smooth. Each breath a gift. Every one of his heartbeats her lifeline.

Gaze glued to the grate, she watched the fire burn. Flickering flames ate through heavy logs. Embers glowed in the near dark. The quiet crackle of a well-laid fire inside the beautiful room should've relaxed her. Allowed her to push past the anxiety while lulling her to sleep. Rannock had warned her she needed it, but no matter how hard she tried, she couldn't shake the feeling something terrible was about to happen.

Cate blew out a long, even breath.

The understatement of the year. Forget about something awful. Something *worse* had already happened.

Adjusting her head on his chest, she pressed her ear over his heart. She listened to the thump, letting the steady rhythm soothe her, then shrugged her shoulder. Worn by time, the soft quilt slid down her arm. She raised her hand. Her fingers slipped through short strands to the nape of her neck. Rubbing back and forth, she imagined what lay underneath her skin. Dread unspooled in the pit of her stomach. Pressing against the spot, she fought through her fears, but...

It was there. Right at the base of her skull. The magical implant that would detonate if she failed to comply.

The Shadow Walkers called it a *pod*. Cate called it extortion—Rathbone's way of controlling Rannock through her. The asshole. How dare he? The guy must be insane. Either that, or what he claimed—desperate. He didn't seem like a bad guy. She got the impression he hadn't wanted to take her, didn't like hurting her, or forcing Rannock into making a deal to protect her. Intuition told her he and Noble—she excluded Dillinger, the jerk—abided by a strict set of principles. At least under normal circumstances.

Too bad everything about her situation screamed *abnormal*.

She was a prisoner with an explosive buried inside her head. But worse, she'd dragged Rannock into her problems, putting him in danger, setting him down in the middle of what amounted to a magical hurricane. Right now, she sat in the eye of the storm. All was calm. All was quiet. But soon, he'd be forced to leave her—inside a house owned by those he now considered enemies, at the mercy of three brothers with supernatural abilities and few scruples, who expected her dragon to go into enemy territory to retrieve what her father stole.

All to save her.

Guilt dug its claws beneath her skin. Remorse followed, joining the parade of if-onlys banging around inside her head. Closing her eyes, Cate swallowed past the lump in her throat.

None of it boded well. Not for her. Not for Rannock, or the other dragon warriors hunkered down inside her studio apartment, waiting for the sun to set and Rannock to move. The entire situation reeked of insanity. She couldn't believe her father's dirty dealings had landed her in trouble. Again. For the... Cate frowned... she couldn't remember how many times she'd bailed him out.

Too many.

Cate clenched her teeth.

Far too many.

If only she'd listened to her sister. Nicole kept telling her to get out of Savannah. The only way to combat their father's tomfoolery was to put distance between them. Cate knew it. Nicole continued to remind her of it, encouraging her to put in her two weeks' notice, pack up her stuff, and move to Scotland.

Fisting her hand in the back of her hair, she turned her face into Rannock's shoulder. Heavy muscles flexed. His hand curled around her hip. Her breath hitched.

God help her.

What had she done?

She should've known better. Talking sense to her father never worked. Trying to keep him on the straight-and-narrow always failed. Being his lifeline only landed her in trouble. At some point a girl had to say *enough*, start looking out for herself, and—

"Catie-mine," Rannock rumbled, interrupting her epiphany.

Yanked from her thoughts, she looked at his face. Dark stubble on a face most guys would kill to possess. Angular cheekbones. Chiseled jaw line. A strong brow below a mess of thick, dark hair. Her chest tightened. So beautiful. Rannock was incredible. Unbreakable spirit. Gorgeous face. Hard body that hid a heart of gold.

"Did I wake you?"

"Your thoughts are verra loud, lass."

She blinked. "You can read my mind?"

He cracked one eye open. "*Bellmia*, we're bonded."

"Energy-fuse," she whispered, recalling what Nicole had told her about the connection she shared with Vyroth. The bond only formed when a Dragonkind warrior met his match. Fueled by dragon DNA and the energy he drew from the Meridian through her, the link lived and breathed inside each couple. The tie that bound—unbreakable, irreversible, intense, and all-encompassing. Stacking her arms on his chest, Cate set her chin on the backs of her hands, went searching and... yeah, right there. She felt him everywhere. In. Out. All around her. "Feels awesome."

"Aye."

"So, you're in my head now." Lifting her hand, she drew her fingertips along his jaw. Day old stubble pricked her skin. "Doesn't seem fair."

"One way tae look at it."

"And the other?"

"Enjoy the idea I know exactly what tae get you for your birthday in two weeks."

An unexpected spark of amusement flicked through her. Grinning, she laughed. "Handy."

"Decidedly." Cradling her in his arm, he shifted in bed. The covers rustled. The mattress dipped as he rolled, turning onto his side, settling her on hers. Sharing a pillow, he kept her close, enclosing her in an enclave as she looked into his eyes. Hazel-orange irises, two golden flecks in his right eye, only one in his left. Pushing his muscular thigh between her own, he brushed long bangs off her face. "You need tae stop stewing, Cate."

"I don't like any of this," she whispered, hooking her knee over his hip.

"I know, but—"

"He's my father, Ran. Always stirring up shit. Always making a mess, then leaving it for someone else to clean up." Her voice hitched. The admission felt like a betrayal, but she refused to lie. She'd been doing it too long. Fixing what she could. Covering up things she couldn't. Denying the truth even when it stared her right in the face. "And now, he's dragged you and your friends into it."

"You as well, Cate."

"I'm his daughter. I'm used to it."

"You shouldnae be," he murmured, drawing gentle circles on her back. "You're a good daughter, Cate. Solid. Loyal. Loving. You should expect the same in return from those you let into your life. Including your sire. A good sire protects his offspring, baby. Yours never has."

So true. Not at all helpful right now.

"I know you're right," she said, heart hurting as the unpleasant truth thumped through her. "But—"

"No *buts*. It's going tae be okay, lass. My packmates and I are powerful on our own. Together, we're near tae unstoppable. If anyone can slip into the Witch's Cauldron undetected and get back out again, 'tis us."

"How do you know Rathbone's telling you the truth?"

"He wants the TriHexe back tae badly tae screw with me. He's given me every scrap of information he has."

"What is it?"

"The TriHexe?"

"Yeah."

"Cannae be sure. Not precisely. I can guess—"

"So guess. I need to know what you know, otherwise I'll go insane when you fly out at sunset."

"I donnae want tae leave you."

"I know."

"Once it's done, I'll come back and take you home."

"I know."

"Stop yer worrying."

"I'll try."

"Nothing's going tae happen tae me."

She hoped not, otherwise...

Her stomach clenched at the thought. She couldn't lose him. Not now. Not ever, but especially after having just found him.

Chewing on the inside of her lip, Cate corralled her dread. "Rannock?"

"Aye."

"What you plan to do is dangerous. Really dangerous, so..." She took a deep breath. "I need you to promise me something."

"What?"

"I know you've decided you have two missions—retrieve the TriHexe and save my father, but—"

"Now who's reading minds?"

"But..." she said, treating him to a pointed look. "If you can't... If you get the TriHexe, but can't get him, don't risk your life for his. I feel like a horrible person just saying it, but I need you to respect my wishes when it comes to my dad."

"*Bellmia,*" he said, thick brogue rolling like thunder.

"I'm serious, Ran." Shattered, hating what she asked him to do, she gripped his wrist to get his attention. "I love my father. He's been the best dad he knows how to be, but he's my past. You're my future."

Rannock murmured her name.

"As much as I love my dad, as much as it'll hurt to lose him, I'll grieve, then survive. But you? I don't think I can live without you now. I need you to come back to me, Ran... no matter what. Do you understand? Tell me you—"

"I understand."

"Thank you," she whispered, then kissed him softly.

She drew away.

He caught her bottom lip between his teeth. A gentle nip. A quick flick of his tongue. His heated gaze collided with hers. "More."

"How much more?"

"Everything, Cate."

"That I can do."

Planting her hand on his shoulder, Cate pushed. Quick to catch on, Rannock rolled onto his back. She went with him, then sat up, settling astride him, baring her breasts, rolling her hips, arching her back... giving him a show.

He growled in approval.

Seeing the need in his expression, she smiled and started to explore, with her mouth, with her hands, with all of her senses. Taking him in, learning what made him purr and growl and groan, storing up memories, ones that would need to last a lifetime if the worst happened, the Witch's Cauldron won, and Rannock never came back to her.

15

Wings spread wide, Rannock rocketed out of thick cloud cover like a demon on fire. Cold air turned warm and humid. A strong updraft buffeted him. Frothing like lava flow, his metallic orange scales glowed in the turbulence. Liquid metal spiraled off the spikes rising along his spine. Molten sparks. One part bronze. Two parts steel. All parts deadly.

He flicked his tail. More embers flew, sparking across the night sky.

Flying above him, Levin dodged. Ice crystals swirled off his frost-blue scales. Snow exploded into a wave of flurries, freezing damp wind mid-gust. The arctic blast blanketed the burning blowback, protecting the ice dragon from overheating.

A good move, particularly since Rannock refused to slow down.

His mission demanded precision. No mistakes could be made. He needed to reach Blood Mountain and find an insertion point into the Blind Witch's court before any of her minions realized he'd infiltrated her nest. A tall order, given the magic he sensed rising in the distance, glimmering over the landscape, hiding in the mist, feasting upon the darkest section of forest. Glamour that provided excellent cover for a coven. Remnants of the Fae. Ones left behind by a Seelie court who'd moved on long ago. Maybe to find greener pastures. Maybe to seek easier prey.

Whatever. The reasons didn't matter.

Only one thing concerned Rannock—the fact the witch had not only found the pocket of Fae magic, but now used it to further her own ends. An excellent strategy. Let someone else do all the work. Jump on the opportunity. Capitalize on the Fae's inattention. Claim territory abandoned to build a safe harbor for witching folk and protect herself from more powerful preternatural hunters.

He admired the effort, appreciated the conservation of energy and recycling of resources. What he didn't like was the Blind Witch's recent foray into the higher levels of magical realms. Her boldness with the Shadow Walkers smacked of arrogance. Tweaking Rathbone's tail didn't make sense. Not for a human witch with limited magical abilities, at least by Dragonkind standards.

Frowning, Rannock blasted over a small town. Pinpricks of light projected into the darkness. He checked his altitude. Twenty-five thousand feet. Plenty of distance between him and the hamlet. Little to be concerned about as he turned his mind back to the conundrum. The witch should've stayed inside the boundary instead of stepping outside it. Magical species from all walks came into the world understanding the hierarchy. Dragonkind sat at the top of the food chain along with the Fae, Shadow Walkers, and the handful of oracles still breathing. Kin in many ways, completely different in others.

Not that it mattered tonight.

The separation between Magickind wasn't his problem. His focus was singular—get in, grab what Rathbone required, get the hell out, and do it in one piece. Otherwise, he wouldn't keep his promise to Cate and return to her before night turned to day. So...

Fuck comfort.

Forget the usual caution.

Spine-bending speed was necessary. So was staying pissed off. His temper served a purpose. A good one. The angrier he got, the more focused he became.

Most Dragonkind males didn't work that way. Levin was a prime example. His packmate worked best, was at his most lethal, when calm. Par for the course for an ice dragon, but the metal in Rannock's blood needed to boil. Calm, cool, and collected meant too relaxed. Too laid-back. Not aware or sharp enough. And with his mate's life on the line, he needed to be as sharp as a samurai's sword.

Banking into a tight turn, Rannock swung north. Molten metal streamed from his wingtips. Twin trails of flame arched across the skyscape.

With a snarl, Levin dove beneath the flux. As he spiraled back up, he threw Rannock another irate look.

A link opened into mind-speak.

"Bloody hell, Ran," Levin said with a growl. *"Shut down the metal works. You want the witch tae see us coming?"*

"You think she's really blind?" Kruger asked, flipping up and over, staying on his wingtip, but well away from flecks of molten steel. *"Or is it meant to be a diversion?"*

Tempel snorted. *"Does it matter?"*

More liquid metal flew.

"Seriously, Ran. Shut that shit down," Levin snapped, swerving to avoid the backsplash. *"You're a living, breathing, flying light show."*

Nothing but the mission on his mind, Rannock ignored his packmates in favor of scanning the rough terrain ahead of him. Chattahoochee National Forest—thick woodland, high elevations, and rugged topography riding the tail end of the Blue Ridge Mountains. Pretty country. Few roads. Even fewer humans around. A six-and-a-half-hour drive from Savannah. Less than an hour flight in dragon form.

Levin sighed.

"I'm cloaked," Rannock said, attention on the shimmer rising over the range. Blue hue. Soft glow. Magic-driven.

"Barely."

Hunting for a weakness in the shield, Rannock angled his wings. Wind shear sliced over his horns. His sonar pinged. Dark orange webbing vibrated as he breathed in, inhaling ancient Fae magic and the smell of pine into his lungs.

He dove toward the canopy.

White contrails joined the burning embers swirling from his wingtips as he levelled out over the treetops. Night vision sharp, he searched the landscape, looking for the insertion point. He'd looked at maps inside Habersham House, studied the terrain, and made a plan. One that provided the best chance of success... and the least time away from Cate.

Ice chips pinged off his scales as Levin flipped up and over. *"Ran."*

"Cloaking spell's tight, Lev. No one can see me." Riding

the wind whistling over the ridge, he scanned the ground. *"Witches included."*

"Metallics," Levin muttered. *"So bloody stubborn."*

Tempel huffed in amusement.

"Know you're angry, lad," Kruger said, emerald-green scales flashing in the bright slash of liquid bronze. Getting as close as he dared, he murmured, understanding how Rannock felt without asking. Not surprising. Brighter than most, Kruger always read him right. *"If I had a mate, I'd hate leaving her too, especially like that, but if you donnae knock it off, you're going tae start a forest fire."*

"Bet humans'll be able tae see that." Ice-blue eyes flashing with temper, Levin threw him a sidelong look. *"All the way from fucking space."*

Tempel grinned, flashing huge fangs.

Clenching his own, Rannock powered down the metalworks. He knew his brothers-in-arms were right, but... man, it was hard to rein in his rage. Almost impossible as he recalled the look on his mate's face when he left her in the bedroom. Naked. Tangled up in sheets infused with his scent. Dark blue eyes full of fear, but not a single tear. Cate kissed him goodbye, but hadn't resorted to crying. He sensed she wanted to, but she'd held on to her composure... for him. So he could do what needed to be done.

His talons twitched.

Pain burned through him as his razor-sharp claws bit into his palm. Goddess help him. Connected to her in elemental ways, he felt what she did while saying goodbye—worry, dread, the burning desire to go with him and help in whatever way she could. Her reaction fueled his, making it nearly impossible for him to walk away.

For him to leave her alone. In a house full of males he didn't trust.

With a snarl, he increased his velocity from scale-rattling to spine-bending.

"Lock it down, Ran," Tempel said, thumping him with the side of his quadruple-bladed tail. Sharp edges met bronze scales. Sparks flew, tumbling between the spikes riding his spine. *"Need you focused."*

"I'm good," he murmured, telling the truth. As always, fury narrowed his focus, drilling down, unearthing his abilities, drawing potent magic up to his surface. The metallic threads in his bloodstream began to bubble. Magnetic force spun deep inside him, seeping through his interlocking dragon skin.

A low hum bled into the air.

Water molecules vaporized.

His vision tunneled as he banked into a wide turn. Spying a break in the blue mist disguising the shield, Rannock shifted in mid-flight. He went wings vertical, tilting, holding a straight line, slicing between towering pines. Wood creaked. Branches swayed. Black in the moon glow, the leafy forage of great oaks rustled as he tightened the cloaking spell keeping him invisible in the sky.

His wingtip cut through the brume. Magic shimmered, bubbling into blue froth.

Slowing his speed, he sank into fog, disappearing beneath the glamour protecting the Witch's Cauldron. The spell swallowed the light. Darkness turned to deep black.

"Single file, lads." Holding steady, disrupting the Fae magic as little as possible, Rannock ghosted over a stream. The brook gurgled. The smell of fresh water swirled. Fog rolled over his scales, painting his scales

with a blue tinge. The forest whispered. He murmured back, mimicking the buzzing sound of insects at work. *"Tail to tail until we land."*

Kruger swung in behind him. Levin and Tempel followed suit, using his wake to hide their numbers.

Silence descended. Black creases became lightening shadows.

Rolling in on a slow glide, Rannock flew over a bluff, then dipped down the other side. Craggy rock opened into a narrow valley. He followed the seam, sliding beneath the attention of watchful eyes.

An owl hooted.

Fish splashed in a nearby stream.

Spotting the opening he needed to set down, Rannock folded his wings. Not a lot. Just halfway, using the webbing to slow his descent. His back paws touched down, not a whisper of sound as his claws carved through compact loam and lose pine needles. Settling into a crouch, he sidestepped, standing guard as his brothers-in-arms landed in the clearing.

Dragon scales rustled.

Mimicking his position, no one made moved as dark magic stroked over ridged scales.

Levin's gaze cut to his.

Rannock shook his head. "*Wait. Let it settle.*"

Tucking his tail around his paws, Kruger searched the western edge of the forest. Tempel looked east as he and Levin took north and south. No one moved. Rannock barely breathed as he and his brothers waited in the gloom in dragon form. The best way to go. Interlocking dragon skin provided more protection than the human variety. And really... why make it easier for the creepers prowling the dark wood?

With his magic up and running, he sensed the sentries from miles away. Creatures created to protect a Fae homestead. Left behind when the colony abandoned the area, the creepers were vicious. No real threat to a warrior in dragon form, but killing the beasts would make noise. A lot of it. Something he wanted to avoid tonight.

Muscles locked, still as a statue, Rannock scanned his quadrant, searching for danger in the darkness. Awash in witchcraft, the forest stood in torment, still and colorless, in sickening tones of grey. A bleak picture. A terrible poisoning. The abiding stench of woodlands long abused and forgotten.

From ten miles away, he heard the creepers turn away from his position. Gaze shimmering, he glanced at his packmate. *"Tempel."*

Magic displaced dank air as Tempel shifted into human form. *"Making a hole."*

Horns tingling, Rannock pushed out of his crouch. *"Quick and quiet."*

Tempel nodded. Arms outstretched, palms facing the forest floor, he turned full circle. One rotation revolved into two, then three. The ground gasped in gratitude, absorbing the male's healing earth magic, then opened, tunneling beneath his packmate's feet. Tempel dropped through the hole.

Arctic air ruffled the trees as Levin shifted and leapt in after him.

Kruger's rough emerald-green scales turned to smooth skin. Conjuring his clothes, he disappeared into the man-sized cavern.

With one last look around, Rannock shifted into human form. Murmuring his wishes, he dressed in his favorite fighting gear, then strode to the edge of the crater. His boots sank into sick, spongy soil. A putrid scent rose around him. Nose twitching, he reached the lip and stared into the vertical shaft.

A straight shot down. Perfect proportions. A round tunnel driving into the bowels of the earth.

Taking a deep breath, Rannock jumped, following his wingmates into the viper's nest.

16

Trapped inside the Emerald Room, Cate stared at the closed door. Solid wood. Honeyed antique patina. No cracks in the raised panels. As beautiful as the rest of the room, but right now, nothing but a barrier—one she must get through if she planned to stay sane tonight.

Sitting cross-legged in the middle of the unmade bed, she picked at her cuticles while contemplating her next move. Her gaze cut to the brass doorknob. First step? Get dressed. Second step? Check to see if the jerks had locked her in. She hadn't heard the lock turn, but that meant nothing. Not with the amount of supernatural hoodoo humming inside the house.

Grabbing the top sheet, Cate dragged it with her as she left the bed. Her bare feet touched down on the oriental rug. She tiptoed around the end of the four-poster monstrosity. Why? No freaking clue. She was alone, at odd ends, about to go out of her mind if she didn't find something to occupy her time until Rannock returned.

No eyes on her as far as she knew, but again... that meant *nothing*.

She didn't know much about Shadow Walkers, but

Rathbone and his brothers didn't seem like the inattentive type.

Rannock hadn't helped on the information front. More interested in making love to her than explaining, he'd skirted her questions about their hosts. Maybe he didn't know. The more likely scenario was he didn't want to scare her. A lovely gesture. She sighed. Her dragon had a heart of gold, even if his reasoning lacked a certain amount of logic.

Ignoring a problem never made it go away. Fear of the unknown only created more uncertainty. A truism, one she could attest to, given she'd been freaked out long before he left her in bed.

Being out of her element tended to do that to her. She liked routine, not the unexpected. A preference no doubt informed by the chaotic nature of her childhood. A shrink would say her father's inability to provide a stable home contributed to her dislike of surprises.

Cate disregarded it all.

She'd survived. Period. No shame in the way she did it, but...

Maybe—just this once—she should embrace the notion of flexibility, given the fluidity of the situation. And the fact she had a pod packed full of explosives inside her head. Bad enough, but worse? Rannock was gone, heading into God-knew-what, to battle blind witches in a cauldron no doubt bubbling with venom.

Another round of fear shivered through her. Unease rose in its wake, making her imagination take flight. Worse-case scenarios kicked up, invading her already unhappy thoughts.

Clutching the sheet to her chest, Cate paused in gathering her clothes. She closed her eyes and sent another prayer heavenward. The tenth—or maybe the hundredth—since Rannock walked out the door, asking for his safe return. She didn't care how he came back to her. All she wanted was to see him again. Hear his voice. Kiss his mouth. Hold him, feel his strong body against hers—forever. Into infinity.

Her hands started to shake.

The belt buckle on her jeans rattled.

Cate opened her eyes. Staring into the banked fire, she shook her head. No way. No how. She refused to fall apart now. Rannock needed her to be strong, to embrace the strain and wait out an untenable situation with fortitude, not fear. To trust him to know what to do and how to take care of himself.

Throwing her clothes onto the armchair, she slipped into her underwear. Jeans and her long-sleeved tee went on next. Her temper began to simmer as she yanked on her socks and glared at the door.

The jerks. Stupid Shadow Walkers. She refused to allow them to intimidate her.

Stomping her feet into her boots, she pivoted and marched toward the door. Prepared to bang it down, she reached for the knob. With a vicious twist, she pulled. The door flew open. Cate lost her grip on the handle. Thrown off balance, she stumbled back into the room and, arms flailing, landed butt-first on the floor.

The thump echoed.

Pain shot up her spine.

"Shit," she said as the door crashed into the wall.

"What the fuck?" a deep voice, full of surprise, growled.

Her attention cut back to the now-open door.

Frozen in the middle of the corridor, Dillinger stared at her. "What the hell are you doing?"

"Losing my frigging mind, apparently."

"Weren't you nuts to begin with?"

"Probably."

A look of consternation crossed his face.

Cate laughed. She couldn't help it. Despite his unpleasant personality, she found him funny. The startled look in his eyes when the door flew open made her night.

"You gonna get up?"

"I'm thinking about it."

Green eyes shimmering, Dillinger scowled at her. "Totally nuts."

"Nah," she said, rolling her feet. "Just in need of a distraction. I can't stay in here. I'll lose my mind."

"So don't," he said, dark brows low. "As long as you stay inside the house, you're golden."

"I know. I just..."

"What?"

"Need something to do."

"Go to the kitchen. Bake something."

Disgust made its way onto her face.

"What about the library?"

She wrinkled her nose.

"The game room?" he asked in a hopeful tone.

Cate pursed her lips.

His eyes narrowed on her. One second ticked into more. Silence stretched, invading her space, filling his. His expression became thoughtful as he contemplated her. He tilted his head, then motioned her out of the room. "Follow me."

She hesitated.

"Not gonna eat you." Glancing over his shoulder at her, he raised a brow. "You want something to keep you busy until your mate returns, move your ass, woman."

Annoyed by his attitude, Cate strode out of the room. "Don't call me *woman*—"

"Aren't you one?"

"—in that tone of voice," she said, ignoring his interruption. "It's patronizing."

She felt him roll his eyes. Seriously. She *felt* it like an invading army crossing hostile borders.

Gaze trained on the back of his head, she trailed Dillinger down the corridor. "You'd think after three thousand years, you'd have learned that lesson by now."

Reaching the top of the stairs, he paused. Intense green eyes met hers. "Three thousand years?"

"Isn't that how old you are?" A clumsy attempt at pulling information out of him, but... so what? She was curious. Self-preservation demanded she play fill-in-the-blanks. "Maybe you're from ancient Egypt."

He snorted.

"Or Mesopotamia. An old dude. Decrepit. Over the hill," she said, poking at him even though she shouldn't. Dillinger wasn't a powder puff. He was a warrior with magical abilities she didn't understand. All the more reason to respect him. Big problem with that assumption. Intuition kept telling her to go the other way. Showing fear never worked when faced with a predator. Better to stand her ground, stare down the devil, and pray she didn't get eaten. "What's that they say?"

"No idea," he murmured, starting down the stairs. "Bet you're going to tell me, though."

"Oh yeah," she said, snapping her fingers. Boot soles tapping against the thick stair runner, she began her descent. Muffled footsteps spiraled, joining his, following the curved stone banister, echoing softly in the enclosed space. "That old dogs can't learn new tricks. Is that the way it is with you?"

"Are you this way with Rannock?"

"Ran gives me orgasms. I'm much nicer to him."

A startled huff escaped him, then he laughed. A rusty sound, scratchy vocal resonance, no doubt stemming from too little use. The rumble echoed in the stairwell, humor transforming his face. Watching him, Cate smiled as laughter settled into a guttural chuckle. Even better. A gorgeous wave of vibrance.

Too bad he didn't indulge in it often.

Nothing but a guess, but she saw the truth in his surprise... and his need to cut his amusement short. Sad, really. A creature of immense power, Dillinger had lived a long time. His deflection when she'd prodded him on the subject proved that well enough. The least he deserved was to find pleasure in everyday things, and be able to laugh with others.

Laughter, after all, was good medicine. And given his disposition, Dillinger needed a serious amount of healing.

The sparkle in his eyes faded. "You're odd, Cate."

"Thank you, Dilly," she said, taking sass out for a spin.

"Jesus."

"Are we going or what?"

Shaking his head, Dillinger swung around a landing and down another set of steps. Cate kept pace, staying three steps behind him, just in case. He might be acting tame now, but no one knew what the future held. One wrong move could set him off. If that happened, she needed to be able to adjust. Run. Hide. Find a safe spot behind a thick door with a solid lock until Rannock arrived to take her home.

Ironic, given she'd just fled a beautiful bedroom and the idea of closed doors.

Following her bad-tempered host, Cate turned another corner. The staircase widened. The smell of fresh wax hit her along with the faintest whiff of motor oil. Her stomach dipped as a shadowed expanse opened in front of her.

A thunk sounded.

Lights started to come on. First, the closest to her. Then the next set and the next, industrial strip lights falling like dominos inside a large garage. An involuntary gasp left her. Three rows of vehicles—one running along the left-hand side, the other to the right, and one straight down the middle. Smooth pillars spaced at even intervals supported an old foundation made of different-colored stone, light and dark grey, some reddish brown, others so pale they appeared almost white.

A gorgeous space. With even better cargo.

Trucks and cars parked in neat rows. Every shape and size and color. Some classic, others space-age new.

"Eureka," she whispered, gobsmacked by the treasure trove.

"My collection," Dillinger said, a half-smile on his face. "My brothers have little interest in automobiles, but I..."

"Have always loved them," she said, knowing what he meant. And would you look at that—she was bonding with a Shadow Walker over well-designed machines. Whoever said hunks of steel didn't possess magic were just plain wrong. "What's your earliest?"

"Benz Patent Motor Car, 1886."

Wow. Very cool. She needed to take a close look at that.

Veering to the left, she walked down one of the aisles, her attention on his collection. "What's your favorite?"

"The Clénet."

"Neoclassic Roadster," she murmured, stopping in front of a 1957 Ford Thunderbird. Gleaming white paint with blood-red leather interior. Slick lines. Low profile. A quintessential classic. "You drive her?"

"Every chance I get."

"Good for you," she said, knowing most collectors didn't. Those who bought the classics she restored never took their "investments" out for a spin. Her clients preferred showrooms, not the open road.

A shame. No matter how expensive, cars were meant to be driven.

Continuing down the line, Cate smiled as she spotted a 1955 Imperial with burgundy paint, a shiny chrome grille, and whitewall tires. "Gorgeous."

"Each one is," Dillinger said, following her progress, making sure she looked, but didn't touch. "But not why I brought you down here."

"Oh?" Turning away from the Imperial, she watched him stroll further down the line.

He stopped in front a vehicle covered in a big tarp. Grabbing the heavy material, he yanked. The grey canvas cover slid to one side, uncovering what lay underneath. Her breath caught. Wow. How pretty. A 1972 Chevrolet Cheyenne K10 pick-up truck. A half-ton, painted the original Hawaiian blue and white, with big, toothy tires.

Unable to resist, Cate crossed the aisle. With an eye on the details, she walked around the pick-up. Ignoring Dillinger's grumble, she ran her hand over the boxy frame and along the hood. Smooth steel. Sleek to the touch. No dimples in the body, or waves in the clear coat. "Body work's good. Who did it?"

"Bought it in this condition."

"Where?"

"Iowa. Some guy had it in his barn."

Figured. The best finds always came from unexpected places: buried under a pile of hay in somebody's barn, forgotten in the back of Great-Granddad's garage, at estate sales when family members finally got around to dusting off a relative's stuff. Or in her case, beat to shit in a field full of old junkers.

Dropping to her haunches, she examined the front grille. "The problem?"

"I can't get it to run."

"Has it ever?"

He shrugged.

She blinked, then popped to her feet. "You've never checked?"

"Arrived on a flatbed. Rolled it in. Haven't moved it since."

Cate opened her mouth to chastise him. Getting a load of his expression, she swallowed the reprimand. "How long have you had it?"

"Twenty-five years."

Staring at him as though he'd lost his mind, she frowned.

"Don't start," he growled. "Just take a look. You wanted a diversion, here it is. Everything you need is against the back wall."

Her attention strayed to the row of standing toolboxes, then moved along the wall. A stack of fender pads to protect precious paint jobs. A couple of mechanic rolling beds leaning against rough stone. Three mobile tool trays milling around. Everything she needed to pop the truck's hood and take a look at the engine.

Excitement skittered through her. Her fingertips started to tingle. "And if I get it running?"

"I'll take the pod out of your skull."

Cate blinked. She turned her head to look at him. "Seriously?"

Dillinger tipped his chin. "Seriously."

"What about your brothers?" she asked, not trusting his offer. "Won't that piss them off?"

"They'll live."

Holding his gaze, Cate chewed on the inside of her lip. "If I do this, you promise to keep your end of the bargain afterward?"

"A word to the wise, Cate." A nasty glint entered his eyes. "I never break my word. Do not question my integrity."

Softly spoken words. Lethal intent behind each one.

Goosebumps erupted on her skin.

Swallowing her unease, Cate nodded once and, leaving Dillinger standing by the Chevy, headed for the toolboxes. "Pop the hood, Dilly. Let's see what secrets she's hiding."

He muttered something under his breath.

Mind already mired in the task ahead, she ignored him. She had a job to do. A pick-up truck to bend to her will. An engine to heal and hear rumble.

Hope spiraled deep, raising her spirits.

Dillinger had just handed her a *chance*. A chance to save herself and help Rannock in the process. The opportunity to influence the outcome of a bad situation and tip the scales in her favor. Determination settled inside her. She could do it. Master the Chevy. Ease Rannock's burden. Save herself.

A lofty goal, but she believed in her skills.

Whether he knew it or not, Dillinger had just handed her the key to the kingdom, one she'd use to open every closed door inside Habersham House. Escaping the Shadow Walkers had been nothing but a pipe dream... before. Now, Cate saw a pathway forward.

Find her way free—eliminate the threat to her life—and the success of Rannock's mission wouldn't matter. Her dragon could abandon his search for the Tri-Hexe. The Shadow Walkers would be forced to do their own dirty work. And she and half the Scottish pack would be airborne, on their way, before Dillinger and his brothers knew what hit them.

Perfect solution to a tricky problem.

Now, all Cate needed to do was pull it off.

17

Vertebrae stacked in a straight line, Rannock jetted down a tube cut through solid bedrock. Feet first. Arms pinned to his sides. Shoulders and arse taking the brunt of the bone-jarring slide.

Fatalistic by anyone's standards, except Olympic athletes participating in the luge event and kamikaze earth dragons.

Tempel loved this shite. Even in the radio silence, he heard the echo of his friend's "*yee-haw!*" through mind-speak as the male rocketed down the tunnel ahead of him.

Gritting his teeth, Rannock hissed as his shoulder scraped the side wall. His jacket dragged across grooves corkscrewing into rock. Metal rivets embedded in the leather sparked against stone. He tightened the cloaking spell surrounding him, ensuring no sound escaped.

A necessary measure.

Fast and silent gave him the best chance of success. Infiltrating the Witch's Cauldron without raising any alarms was a tall order.

The second she realized her coven had been

breached, things would go from bad to worse. Getting in under the wire required a certain amount of savvy, and a helluva lot of finesse. The longer he went undetected, the better for him and the warriors with him. Even if meant riding Tempel's subterranean deathtrap.

Rocketing around a corner, Rannock checked his position. The tunnel narrowed, growing even steeper, dragging him deeper underground. His speed increased. Cursing under his breath, he fine-tuned his sonar. A ping echoed inside his head as his spine screamed in protest. Shoving the discomfort away, he zeroed in, tracking his packmates' progress.

Three blips blinked onto his mental screen. Almost there. Another quarter mile. In less than a minute he'd drop into the corridor where his brothers-in-arms already stood, boots planted, hackles up, deep in darkness, waiting for him to arrive.

Tense in anticipation, Rannock prepared to put on the brakes. He didn't want to do it, really wanted to avoid the physical fallout, but some things couldn't be helped. Pain was nothing but sensory input. The body's way of protesting, but... mind over matter. No matter how much it hurt, he needed to slow his velocity. Otherwise, he'd torpedo out the end of Tempel's tunnel and go splat inside the witch's lair. Not optimal, given the need for quiet.

Starting the countdown, Rannock got ready. Speed at smash-scale levels, he bent his knees and planted his heels. Rigid boot soles ground into rock. Dust kicked up. The smell of burning rubber rose in the compact space. His velocity slowed, but...

Not enough.

Gritting his teeth, he slammed his forearms into the side of the tube. Leather moaned. Twin zippers shrieked. The cacophony bounced around inside the cloaking spell. His head started to buzz as the high-pitched whine battered his eardrums. Choking on stone dust, Rannock bore down, using every inch of his six-foot-eight, two-hundred-and-sixty-pound frame. The spine-ripping speed downgraded another notch. He pressed harder, steady pressure, making minute adjustments, increasing the resistance as he saw light at the end of the tunnel.

The bottom dropped out.

Solid rock became open air.

His feet swung free. His body flew through the man-sized hole.

About to jet into the void, he grabbed for the edge. His hands caught and held. Momentum straightened his arms, then reversed, yanking him backward. Ligaments stretched. Taut muscles pulled. Pain stabbed him as his elbows jerked, bringing him to an abrupt stop.

Hanging from the ceiling, he swayed in the low light. A dust cloud swirled into the open expanse below him. The scent of lamp oil tickled his nose. With a grunt, he solidified his grip and, clinging to grooves in the stone, sent his senses searching.

Fine filaments of magic spun into a web. He threw it like a net. Metal ions transformed into magnetic force, rushing over the walls, ceiling, and floor, coating everything it touched. Gathering the threads, he pulled on the strings, drawing the whisper-thin cables to him, reading the information embedded in the fibers.

Two miles underground. A complex warren of interconnected corridors and rooms. Elven-made structure commissioned by the former residents of a Seelie court. Once abandoned, now smoldering with dark magic. He smelled the distillation, the slow boil of Fae power turning into something less powerful, but far more sinister.

A quiet tap sounded below him.

Sensing his packmates, Rannock abandoned his perch. He hung suspended in midair a moment, then dropped fifty feet to the floor. His boots thumped against stone. His knees rebounded, softening his landing.

Silence descended. His night vison sparked.

A metallic orange glow washed into a wide corridor as he looked around. Cracked mosaic tiles beneath his feet. Vaulted stone ceiling above his head. Immense columns standing with their backs to the wall at even intervals along both sides of the long hall. Elaborate murals between each pair. Peeling paint. Colors faded by time. Historical depictions no doubt long forgotten by the Fae who'd once lived inside the underground complex.

Listening for footfalls, Rannock shifted toward the side wall. Low light flickered from lamps set inside cast-iron holders bolted to the walls. Deep shadows seethed between pools of illumination. Eerie echoes. The quiet chant of voices came from far away. Very medieval. No magic in the lantern flames, though. A pain to maintain. Which meant someone filled the lamps with oil on a regular basis.

The Blind Witch's minions, maybe. A group that might already be making the rounds.

Narrowing his focus, Rannock scanned for any life forms. No human sweat on the faint breeze. Muted witchling magic. The shifting stench of rotting flesh in the air. Lots of bad vibes, but little to be concerned about right now. All was quiet. No one but him and his brothers inside the long corridor, or the ones connected to it.

Dragon half aligned, magic at the ready, Rannock rolled his shoulders, shrugging off the last of his discomfort. He glanced to his left.

Ice-blue eyes stared out of the shadows.

Without making a sound, he followed Levin's lead and conjured more gloom. Musty air swirled around him. The cloaking spell deepened. As he disappeared inside a web of invisibility, Rannock sidestepped, putting his back to the wall. Looking both ways, he met Kruger's yellow-green gaze, then shifted focus. He tipped his chin at Tempel. Earth dragon mojo up and running, he raised his hand. Index finger against his mouth, he shook his head, warning Rannock not to use mind-speak.

Good call.

The quieter, the better. Less chance of detection that way. More time for reconnaissance. Better odds of grabbing the TriHexe and making it out of the witch's nest with all his scales intact.

Using hand signals, Rannock called the play and, staying low, moved down the corridor. Intuition bubbled to the surface. His dragon half filled in the gaps. Magnetic force seeped into the hollows like plaster poured into a mold, then solidified, supplying him with a layout of the subterranean complex. He drew the map to the front of his mind and, using foreknowledge to his advantage, navigated the twists and turns.

One corridor spun into the next, some full of hand-carved pictographs depicting battles fought before Christ was born, others plain, with rough walls. Pausing on the lip of a large vestibule, he re-scanned and crept down a shallow set of stairs, past towering pillars, under a gilded coffered ceiling, deeper into the enemy lair.

Taking the steps two at a time, he mounted the other side. Bracketed by columns, he stepped onto the landing. He glanced at the wall acting as a dead end. Two choices—go left, or turn right. Looking one way, he went the other and—

The chanting increased in volume and tempo.

Flames in the hanging lanterns blew out.

Bright blue light washed in, coming from the opposite end of the corridor.

Squinting, Rannock shuttered his night vision, protecting his light-sensitive eyes, but kept moving. Floating like sprinkles in the air, the brilliance expanded, showing him the way. He followed the shimmer. The corridor ended, dumping him onto the lip of a balcony.

Wide and deep, the mezzanine ran around the outside of a circular chamber. Voices rolled up from down below, echoing beneath a domed ceiling. More delicate gold work on smaller Corinthian columns. Different murals on the walls—battle scenes from a Fae war fought over a millennium ago. A brutal mix of two different kinds of magic in the room, one light, the other dark.

Crouched in the shadows, Rannock searched the balcony for the enemy. No witches on the upper level, just statues of vicious-looking Foo Dogs staring down into the chamber. Moving slowly, Rannock slid onto his belly. Flat on the floor, he army-crawled toward the railing.

Bright light burned brighter. Voices raised in worship grew louder. The stink of black magic tightened its grip on the room.

His dragon half reacted, recoiling in disgust. Bile

touched the back of his throat. Clinging to control, Rannock swallowed the burn and stopped at the edge of the balcony. Kruger and Tempel on one side of him, Levin on the other, he peered through slots in the banister, down into a large, Romanesque amphitheater, and—

Nearly got blinded.

With a silent curse, he turned his head away.

Seeing spots, he closed his eyes, reset his shields, then looked back toward the object stationed on the lowest level, in the center of the theater floor. Set on a high stand inside a pentagram drawn with chalk on black marble inlay, resting on a bed of solid gold, a crown of interconnected hexagons shone with piercing intensity. Three were large, anchored by four smaller ones resting between them. All burning bright. All losing power.

His attention shifted to the female standing a safe distance away.

Naked, a red robe pooled on the floor at her feet, long black hair falling over her sickly pale skin, a witch raised her hands toward the TriHexe. Blue light pulsed. Magic bled from each hexagon as she chanted, invoking a draining spell. Her minions gathered around her, some seated in the stands, others bare and kneeling in a circle around her and the TriHexe. Heads bowed, males and females swayed together as they repeated her words, and she sucked Rathbone's property dry.

His focus returned to the TriHexe. Metal exoskeleton. Simple construction. The power to destroy worlds contained inside it.

His eyes narrowed. As a Metallic, he should be able to touch it without dying. The metal alloy in his blood would protect him if he made contact. Or at least should—in theory. No way to know for sure, but...

Maybe if he conjured a container to put around it. Constructing a carrying case might buy him the time he needed, protect him during transport, just long enough for him to fly back to Savannah and set it in Rathbone's hands.

Needing to be sure, Rannock tapped into the Tri-Hexe's energy. He poked around the edges. A wave of soothing magic surged, ebbing into flowing current. Drawing the rich scent into his lungs, he shifted through molecules, tasting the vintage, trying to identify the source of its power.

The chanting grew stronger.

The TriHexe flickered.

His packmates tensed beside him.

Rannock understood the reaction. The TriHexe was so powerful, it could kill his kind, obliterate him with a single pulse. And yet Rannock didn't stop. He mined the energy, sipping it like fine Scotch. Dissecting, cataloguing, discovering its flavor as he explored the immense energy.

The magic inside spooled into three different threads.

His nostrils flared.

Fucking hell.

The scent of Shadow Walkers. The trio's signature was everywhere, written in code inside the TriHexe, under the dome, seeping up the stairs, along the balcony into the corridor behind him.

The insistent pulse invaded his muscles and bones. His tension eased, and realization struck. Rannock shook his head. Even after having met the Rathbone and his brothers, he never would've guessed. But magic didn't lie... and the source of the Shadow Walkers' power spoke volumes.

Older than the Fae and Elven races, the Triad Rathbone commanded helped hold the world together. Weavers of experience, in a sense. Healers of psyche, in another. A warrior race, keepers of every species, the maintenance crew who ensured the electrostatic bands ringing the planet—source of all living things, and the energy that nourished Dragonkind—kept humming.

Nearly extinct, few remained in the world. Which explained a lot—like why humans were forever at each other's throats and the earth slipped deeper into the grip of environmental disaster every year.

Frowning, he glanced at his brothers-in-arms.

Intense yellow-green eyes met his as Kruger shook his head.

Levin bared his teeth.

Tempel mouthed, *Fuck*.

Rannock agreed.

The stakes had just been raised. Aborting the mission if things got hairy was no longer an option. Rathbone and his Triad required the TriHexe. What the Shadow Walkers did with it was anyone's guess. Might be for the trio's continued good health. Could be Rathbone needed it to accomplish the ancient task entrusted to him by the Goddess of All Things, or to finish weaving connectivity back into the world.

Didn't matter.

Right now, Rathbone's reasons were irrelevant. Rannock might find out what he used it for later, or he might not. Whatever. For now, only one thing mattered. He must move to protect the TriHexe before the Blind Witch consumed what little magic remained.

Shifting, he settled into a crouch. Balanced on the balls of his feet, he stared at the warriors beside him.

Each one nodded.

Good to go. Not a hint of hesitation.

With a growl, Rannock set his hand on the railing. Muscles cranked tight, he leapt up and over. His feet cleared the stone lip. Ripping free of the cloaking spell, he plunged into the Witch's Cauldron, roaring as the Blind Witch spun to face him.

White eyes devoid of color met his gaze. She hissed, flashing blackened teeth filed into sharp points.

Her minions shrieked, letting out a battle cry.

Landing hard, Rannock conjured twin war axes and entered the fray. No time could be wasted. Mission now trumped all. The very fabric of the world depended on it.

18

Boots sliding across the floor, Rannock dove beneath a wave of black magic. Tucking his head, he somersaulted across the upper gallery. His shoulder rolled over smooth concrete. The toxic brume streamed over his head. A single revolution and he was on his feet, ready to fight. Prepared to annihilate and protect the TriHexe as its pulse weakened three flights below.

Rotating the war axes in his hands, he snarled at the witch standing in the center of the amphitheater. A series of steep stairs between him and her—no easy way to reach her unless he shifted into dragon form.

Kicking the robe at her feet out of the way, she shifted into a fight stance in front of the TriHexe. Hands raised, fingers curled like claws, her white, sightless eyes drilled into his.

"Dragons," she hissed, razor teeth flashing.

"Witch," he growled back, aggression swirling in his veins.

Painted blood red, her lips curved. "Rathbone... always the clever one."

Her voice slithered through open air, inciting violence.

The urge to uncage his beast raged through him. He wanted to accommodate her and unleash hell. Destroy her, then turn his magic on her minions, ensuring she never ventured beyond her coven again. Instinct stopped the impulse. Something about the setup bothered him. Something Rathbone mentioned warned him.

As powerful as he and his brothers were, none could enter the underground warren. Which told him the magic inside could damage the Shadow Walkers, ruin the males in some way. Poison each one, leave lasting effects if it didn't kill them first. Strange. More than a touch alarming. The conclusion might be right, but made very little sense, unless...

His eyes narrowed, he stared at the witch.

She was too still. Frozen in place as she watched him. As though waiting for something to happen.

What exactly?

Excellent question. One he must answer before shifting into dragon form. Holding her gaze, he bared his teeth. His fangs elongated. His fingernails morphed into sharp claws. More catlike than Dragonkind, but good enough to provoke a response as he unleashed his own voice, roaring at her.

White eyes aglow, she screamed back, revealing two rows of serrated teeth. Sound waves shot from her mouth. Putrid air warped, blurring his vision right before the invisible pulse struck the middle of his chest.

Oxygen disappeared. His lungs contracted. Pain rippled around his ribcage.

She screamed again.

The second concussive wave hammered him. The blast threw him backward. His feet left the floor. He slammed spine-first into the wall. Concrete crumbled. A cloud of dust rolled into the air. The punishing pulse pushed him deeper into stone. Pinned four feet off the floor, he kept his eyes open and his war axes raised as smoke filled the amphitheater. Thick curls billowed up the stairs.

The Blind Witch stopped screaming. Sound waves disappeared. Dropping to the floor, Rannock hunted for the witch in the chaos. She sank deeper into the smoke, obscuring his view of her.

Smart move.

The brume hid her well, making it almost impossible for him to track her from his position above the theater floor.

Weapons at the ready, he lunged toward the lip of the gallery. The stench of black magic filled his lungs. Bile sloshed against the back of his throat. Again. He'd lost count of the number of times in the last hour. The toxic mix hit him again. He gagged. Hellfire, she stank in ways he'd never smelled before, ways that signaled trouble for him and his brothers-in-arms.

Forcing himself to take another drag, Rannock shifted through the complexities. The taste washed over his tongue. His stomach pitched. Refusing to give up the hunt, he stayed with it, separating the components. Some witchling magic derived from incantations. Some power drawn from the TriHexe. But the other third—pure Fae magic.

"Shite," he rasped, exhaling toxins from his lungs.

She was a hybrid, one in control of black magic fueled by a powerful bloodline. Which limited his options. No way could he shift into dragon form now. Allowing his beast out to play was too dangerous. Any other time, in any other situation, he wouldn't have hesitated, would've used teeth, claws, tail, and exhale to annihilate the witch's coven. But after reading the air and tasting the magic? No fucking way. Too much toxicity hung in the air.

And hidden inside it, a stealing spell, one designed to trap him.

He smelled the incantation, sensed the darkness hovering just under the dome, waiting to strike, just like the witch. The instant she saw his dragon, she'd drop a net over him, steal his power straight from the source.

The realization strung him tight.

Spinning toward his packmates, Rannock shouted a warning.

Busy fighting, none responded.

Pivoting, he raised his war axes and, meeting the enemy horde streaming over the top step, reached out with his mind. The link opened, connecting him to his brothers-in-arms. "*Donnae shift! Donnae—*"

"What?" Battling four witches at once, Levin swung twin ice swords. Frosty blades bit into once-human flesh turned something else. Black blood flew, splattering across pale stone.

Magic frothing, seconds away from shifting, Kruger growled.

Panic tightened its grip. *"Ruger—stop!"*

Yellow eyes aglow, Kruger hesitated. *"Why?"*

"She's mixed blood. Half Fae, half Witchling."

"So?" Dark eyes shimmering with unholy light, Tempel raised rock mallets the size of Thor's hammer. Stone struck bone, splitting a minion's head wide open. Spinning to face another, he bared his teeth. *"What does it matter to us?"*

Fighting back-to-back with his brothers, Rannock rotated into a smooth spin. The enemy crested the last step. Five across, three deep, weapons aimed at him, the horde swarmed.

He struck, slicing through flesh and bone. Bred inside the coven, demon witches dropped at his feet. More of the Blind Witch's minions streamed up the stairs into the gallery, long hair flying behind each one. Blades shimmering bronze in the TriHexe's glow, he swung his double-sided war axes over and over, again and again. Striking with precision. Spinning beneath glinting swords and gleaming knives. Avoiding the sharp bite of poison-tipped steel claws his enemy wore.

Demon witches howled. Black blood flew. Head after head rolled. More magic-driven smoke spilled over the steps.

"Ran," Kruger snapped.

Hunting for the Blind Witch in the chaos, Rannock kicked a witch off the end of his axe. *"The room is wrapped in a stealing spell. The second you shift—"*

Levin cursed. *"She'll corrupt our magic and—"*

"Kill our dragon halves," Kruger said, raising his hands. Poisonous gas spilled from his palms and billowed down the stairs. The horde climbing toward him gasped. Seconds later, all lay dead, limp bodies littering the lower levels of the amphitheater.

"Jesus fuck," Tempel snarled, splitting heads, only to have more surround him. *"There are too many of them. And more are coming."*

War axes whirling, Rannock spun full circle. Battle-sharpened blades bit into neck muscles and cut through. Heads toppled, one after the other, bouncing down the steps to reach center court. Blood flew from his axes as he pivoted to face the next wave flying up the steep stairs. *"How many?"*

With a flick of his wrist, Tempel threw one of his hammers. The huge mallet spun like a boomerang, arching wide, knocking minions off the lip of the gallery. As the horde fell down the stone steps, the hammer returned to him. *"Too many to count."*

With a snarl, Rannock reset his stance. A male lunged over the last step and plunged onto the gallery. Poison-tipped claws raised, he howled at Rannock. Crazed eyes met his a second before he flew at him. An instant, a single beat was all it took for Rannock to recognize the human planning to attack him.

Henry Biscayne.

His mate's sire under the unbreakable influence of a witch with no mercy.

"Fuck," he said between clenched teeth as Cate's father ran toward him, wild-eyed, dark blond hair matted, eyes the same color as Cate's full of battle fury.

Guard raised, Rannock rotated the axe in his hand and waited. Killing her sire was out of the question. Cate didn't want him risking his life for the male, but now that Rannock faced him, he'd be damned if he didn't bring the bastard home to her.

Henry raised his fist and swung.

Rannock dodged the deadly tips of his steel claws. Time slowed down. His focus narrowed. The fighting moved from fast to slow motion. He counted off the seconds. Three. Two. One...

Henry lunged at him again.

Rotating his axe, Rannock bashed him in the side of the head, blades turned away, flat side deployed. Metal and wood cracked against the side of Henry's skull. Dazed but not cut, he stumbled sideways... and Rannock made his move.

Grabbing the front of Henry's shirt, he yanked him forward, slamming his elbow into the male's temple. Henry went limp. Rannock tossed Cate's unconscious sire behind him. He landed in a heap on the floor.

Kruger jolted. *"What the hell?"*

Rannock sliced through another witch. *"He comes with us."*

"Who the hell is it?" Tempel asked, slipping on blood, trying not to trip over Henry.

"My mate's sire."

"Fucking hell, brother" Kruger murmured. *"You always gotta be the hero."*

"Bugger off," he muttered, fighting off three males at once.

"Time to go." Hacking at his attackers, ice chips flying from the tips of his swords, Levin bumped into Rannock. *"Grab the TriHexe, Ran."*

Battling to stay on his feet, Rannock fought his way closer to the stairs. *"The Blind Witch."*

Kruger snarled. *"Forget about her. She's already gone."*

"I want her head. I want—"

"Ran," Levin said, stabbing the enemy with an ice dagger.

"Fuck. All right." Lopping off another head, wishing it was the Blind Witch's, Rannock turned toward the TriHexe. *"Tempel—find us a way out."*

"Digging," Tempel said, turning toward the amphitheater's outer wall. *"Watch my six."*

Hands raised, Kruger conjured a wall of poison fog. Keeping it between him and the horde, he abandoned his position, moving to protect Tempel's back. *"Got you."*

"Brace, lads," Rannock said.

Holding the line, Levin grunted. *"Just get it done."*

Tempel started burrowing. The deafening sound of drilling roared across the gallery, drowning out screams as plaster dust joined the smoke in the air.

Ground shaking beneath his feet, Rannock turned

inward. Body fending off the demon horde, mind focused on the TriHexe, he conjured a holding container. Solid steel with bronze threads. Nine layers thick. Strong enough to contain an exploding bomb. Big enough to set the TriHexe inside, rendering it safe for transport.

Metal threads spinning in open air, he knitted the six-sided box together. Calling on his dragon half, he raised his hand and summoned the TriHexe. The metal in the magical device obeyed his command. The crown of hexagons levitated, rising above the golden cradle on top of the tripod.

Rannock flicked his fingers.

Moving like a missile, the TriHexe flew in his direction, up the stairs, over corpses, above the blood streaming across stone. Bracing for impact, he tucked one of his war axes back into the weaponry inside his mind and opened the box. The crown slammed into steel. The container rammed into his chest. Metal shrieked. Magic detonated like a bomb. Blown off his feet, Rannock flew backward. Battling the pain, he scrambled to close the lid.

One of the latches slipped.

Cracked open from the impact, pure power leaked from the TriHexe, billowing into his face, stealing his air, seeping into his muscles and bone. His vision flickered. His mind went blank. His dragon half turned away, sinking inside him.

Kruger shouted his name.

Too little, too late.

He was already gone, falling deep into a darkness so complete, Rannock knew he'd never find his way back out.

19

Key ring in hand, Rathbone wandered out of the study. He stopped beneath one of the soaring tri-arches and glanced up at the mother-of-pearl inlay. A unique design, elaborate carvings depicting the history of his Triad. All the feuds. All the near misses. One pearl added for every battle fought.

Seemed a strange place to put it. He hadn't argued, though, when Dillinger insisted.

The past always informed the future. And like it or not, seeing his history every time he walked into the study wasn't a bad thing. Most days, the layout reminded him to tread lightly, go wisely, move through the world in the way of his kind—with a whisper, not a heavy hand. Today, however, seeing the display only made his stomach clench and his temper boil.

He didn't like allowing others to fight his battles for him. Wasn't built to stand on the sidelines or turn away from the fray.

He liked action. Wanted battle. Needed the outlet to calm the raw elements of his nature. Flexing his hand around the keys, Rathbone released a ragged sigh. It had been so long, too goddamned long since his steel had seen battle. Without release, the power inside him writhed, begging to be used, unleashed in the ways of the old world.

Back then, finding someone to kill had been easy. These days, not so much. Which made sending Rannock and his warriors to infiltrate the Witch's Cauldron, instead of going himself, all the more irksome.

The second he grabbed Cate, his conscience started singing.

The moment he met Rannock, guilt joined the chorus.

Now, a whole choir of doubt occupied his mind.

Keeping a male from his female was never right. Blackmailing one by threatening his mate bordered on unconscionable. Dillinger never said much, but he could tell his brother didn't like it either. Noble kept telling him it had been necessary. He was no doubt right, and yet...

And yet...

The whole mess bothered Rathbone. Probably more than it should, given the dragon warrior's level of lethal.

Twirling the ring in his hand, Rathbone glanced over his shoulder into his favorite room. Keys hit the center of his palm. Metal jangled against metal as he stared at the fire.

Fed by his magic, flames roared against the iron grate. No wood. Zero kindling. Not a scrap of paper to be seen. Just the fire in the pit of his belly made manifest by the turmoil in his mind. Destructive, perhaps, but he needed the outlet, a way to drain the potent magic slithering beneath the surface of his skin.

Without the TriHexe in its cradle, he had nowhere to channel the excess, no way to manipulate to the Meridian in order to shape and polish the power. Just overload and excess, malnourishment and pain. Worse, his brothers suffered right alongside him, amplifying the current, adding to the torture.

Dillinger became more volatile by the minute. And Noble... Rathbone clenched his teeth. Goddamn him. Feeling the burn, his brother withdrew, closing himself away, fearing the fallout if his nature spilled out of bounds.

Which left him here, twiddling his thumbs, while worry sliced him raw and rage picked at his bones.

Fisting his hand around the keys, Rathbone stepped out from beneath the arches. Cushioned by antique rugs, he strode down the corridor into darkness. Extinguished candles reacted to his mood. Flames sparked on dry wicks and illumination spilled as he moved deeper into his home buried beneath Habersham House.

He rarely went abovestairs anymore. No need. The boutique hotel he owned didn't need him. He employed humans for such tasks. Those who rented his rooms and slept in beds secure behind locked doors, beneath the roof he provided, were well treated, filling his coffers with borrowed money it would take years for them to pay back.

No reason to mess with a good thing.

So he didn't, unless his manager e-mailed him about a problem she couldn't solve. A rarity, thank the goddess. He wanted to deal with humans about as much as he wanted to be eaten by Dillinger in beast mode.

Reaching a locked door, he drew the pad of his thumb over the keys in his hand. Metal ridges stroked his skin. He rotated the ring again, listened to the jangle, wondering why he carried the jumbled mess. Noble kept asking. Rathbone never provided a response. Maybe he did it to annoy his brother. Maybe the habit soothed him somehow. Mostly, though, he didn't know why he needed a drawer full of keys.

Key ring snug against his palm, he murmured, voicing his wishes.

Complicated locking mechanisms clicked. Multiple deadbolts slid to one side. The vault door swung open, bumping against the wall.

Ducking beneath the low lintel, Rathbone strolled onto a wide landing, then down a set of steps. Stale air once brimming with magic met him on the way down. He swallowed his annoyance, recognizing his response for what it was—grief. He missed the TriHexe like he would an amputated limb, like a loved one, forever lost to the misfortunes of time.

He tightened his grip on the cluster of keys and, forcing himself to keep walking, rounded the corner. He paused and peered into the crypt. Built centuries ago, the six-sided chamber rooted his house to the ground. The seat of power for his kind. The place where the TriHexe had sat for over three hundred years after he and his brothers made the trip from West Africa to North America.

Early days on the new continent. The good old days, some of his kind insisted.

Rathbone didn't really care. After two-and-a-half thousand years spent roaming the earth, time meant very little anymore. With a blink, one hundred years passed like dust blown across a desert, nothing but sand spun through an hourglass. Little more than long days and lonely nights spent in a city chosen for—

Raw energy rippled beneath the surface of his skin.

Rathbone flinched.

The base where the TriHexe usually sat pulsed.

Bright light flashed across the crypt, flaring across pictograms carved into the marble-clad walls. Sparks burst from the cradle's prongs. Shimmers exploded upward, puffing against the gilded ceiling.

Surprise turned to awe, then morphed into gratitude.

Rathbone sucked in a quick breath. The TriHexe was close. Less than ten miles away, moving fast, closing in on Habersham House with speed and intensity. Reaching across the distance, the power called to him as it returned home.

Spinning away from the golden base, Rathbone raced across the chamber toward the stairs. He reached out with his mind, tracking the TriHexe, tapping into each dragon warrior's unique energy signal. Unable to tell the dragons apart from a distance, he read the force of their magic. Four distinct energy signatures appeared on his mental grid. Three healthy and whole, but the last...

Rathbone frowned.

He narrowed his focus and—

"Christ," he growled as the problem came to light.

One of the four was injured... badly. Unconscious. Thready pulse. Suffering from serious energy depletion. A state that would kill the Dragonkind warrior if he didn't feed, and do it fast.

Unease crept in to replace his elation.

He brushed it aside as a fifth heartbeat registered on his grid. Surprise spun him around the lip of reality. Jesus. A human. The dragon warriors flew toward Habersham House with a *human* in tow, one suffering from magic sickness—the kind Rathbone knew at a glance couldn't be cured.

With a curse, he took the stairs three at a time.

His feet touched down on the landing. He snarled at the door. The heavy panel slammed open. Avoiding the backlash, he roared over the threshold into the hallway.

A loud thump rippled down the main corridor. Dark eyes with yellow fire glowed from the opposite end of the hallway. "Rath—incoming!"

"I feel it," he yelled back, answering Noble's call. "Where's Dillinger?"

"With Cate in the garage."

Shock whipped through him. Another round of dread followed. "What the fuck?"

"He hasn't hurt her."

"Yet," he snapped, blood rushing through his veins. Worry for Rannock's mate throbbed through him. "What were you thinking? You promised to keep track of him."

"He likes her." Jogging a fast clip, Noble met him in front of the tri-arches.

"All the more reason to keep him the hell away from her. Jesus, Noble." Sliding to a stop, Rathbone stared his brother. He'd clearly lost his mind. No other explanation. Leaving Cate with Dillinger amounted to setting a helpless lamb down in front of a hungry lion.

Noble opened his mouth, no doubt to defend his decision.

He sliced his hand through the air. "Never mind. Get to the crypt. Prepare the chamber. I'll join you with Dillinger after I see to Cate."

Concern in his dark eyes, Noble hesitated. "One of them's injured."

"It better be Rannock."

"Why?"

"The injured male needs an immediate infusion of

energy—right from the source," Rathbone said. "Cate's high energy, and given the extent of the injuries I sense, she's the only one with a strong enough connection to the Meridian to feed him. Anything less, and he won't survive. Even with her, he might not live."

"And?"

"A Dragonkind warrior never shares his mate, Noble. Packmate or not, Rannock will attack anyone who touches her," he said, imagining the worse, preparing for the fallout. "I don't want dead dragons in my foyer, do you?"

"Fuck no."

"Then get moving. We've got work to do."

"Call me if you need help controlling the dragon horde."

Rathbone nodded.

Slapping him on the shoulder, Noble sprinted down the hall toward the crypt.

With a sharp pivot, he ran in the opposite direction. He needed to reach the garage before Rannock and his brothers landed at the side entrance… and Dillinger made things worse by hurting Cate.

20

With the hood propped up and engine on display, Cate attached the socket to the extension rod. Leaning over one of the fender pads protecting the custom paint job, she disappeared under the hood and, ratchet wrench in hand, tightened a bolt. One crank turned into two, then three. The fifth time, however, was the charm, settling the bolt head snug against the steel frame. The last one in a long series of loose nuts and stripped bolts.

She'd done the rounds, tightening some, replacing others.

Setting the tool aside, she popped the cap off the top of a spark plug and pulled the boot. One started. Seven more to change.

Working at a steady pace, she removed one plug at a time, then replaced each in order, measuring the gap, applying grease to the ceramic core, screwing each one into their designated well. The zip of the torque wrench rose through the quiet. The sound settled her in ways little else ever did.

Nicole called her a grease monkey. Cate knew her sister wasn't wrong.

From the moment she could hold a wrench, she'd been ripping stuff apart and putting it back together. Radios. Old refrigerators. Lawnmowers, boat motors, and abandoned go-carts. Cars, though, had always gotten her motor running.

From the age of fourteen, she'd drifted through the scrap yard her father managed to provide cover for his "real job." The acres of wreckage had provided countless hours of entertainment, mostly by helping her avoid her father's schemes... and the men he choose as his associates.

The second she turned sixteen, she applied for a job at every garage in town. Most blew her off. Kane gave her a chance, teaching a girl what most men never would, providing a refuge after school and on weekends, keeping her sane in the face of her dad's nonstop cons, and helping her find her calling.

Her dad had called it a phase, hoping she'd join the family business. But her fascination with classic cars only deepened.

Which explained her current situation—trapped inside a house owned by Shadow Walkers, and still, somehow, she managed to get grease on her hands and find her way under the protective cove of a raised hood.

The work settled her nerves, helping her concentrate on the task at hand, instead of worrying about Rannock. Cate huffed as she turned the torque wrench. Stupid, really, to even try. Not thinking about him was an impossibility. Her dragon was always top of mind, in her thoughts, in her prayers. So deep inside her heart, she hurt every time it beat. Now her chest ached and her mind burned. An internal inferno of fear.

For him. For her. For the loss of a future she

wanted, but might never get to have if he didn't come back.

She inhaled deep, then exhaled slow, allowing the quiet to seep into her bones. The scent of motor oil drifted. The ratchet in her hand zinged. A ticking clock called out each second, helping her sink deeper into the job. Smooth metal beneath her grease-stained hands. Mechanical components she knew how to rip apart and put back together. A way to make things whole when nothing else felt right.

Focused on the last spark plug, she twisted it into place, trying to forget Rannock and his brothers were out there somewhere, battling supernatural creatures she hadn't known existed before tonight and didn't want to understand. Surreal was a good term for the world she now inhabited. Batshit crazy was another. But right now, beneath the cage light hooked to the underside of the hood, all she felt was scared.

Scared for Rannock. Worried for herself. Concerned about the fact Dillinger watched her from less than ten feet away.

Her instincts flickered, threatening to upend the calm she'd worked hard to cultivate. Flexing her hand around the tool grip, she battled a second, forcing her stomach to settle and her mind to stay on task. Just a few more adjustments to make, a couple more caps to click into place. After that, it would be time to pay the piper, to see if her hard work had paid off and Dillinger kept his word.

She wanted the pod out of her head. She wanted to set eyes on Rannock again. She wanted the hell out of Savannah and away from the craziness.

Terrific goals. Iffy outcome. No way to know which way the situation would swing and the universe would toss her.

Cate swallowed, trying to loosen the knot in the center of her chest. So many wants. Just as many needs. All within reach, and yet still too far away to touch.

Inspecting her work, she twisted the wrench a quarter turn, then nodded. Perfect fit. Easy installation. All the rusty spark plugs removed. Clicking the caps and wires back in place, she reattached the intake valve, fighting to stay calm as Dillinger shifted a few feet away.

His silence cranked her the wrong way. Especially after the last couple of hours.

He'd talked almost nonstop, watching her with an intensity she didn't like, refusing to leave her alone inside the garage, asking questions (personal as well as car-related), keeping her on edge as she worked on his truck. He'd done it on purpose, poking, prodding, gauging her reactions, smiling a little when she lost her patience and snap at him.

The jerk.

She'd started out liking him. Now, she couldn't decide what she wanted to do more—stab him with a screwdriver or kneecap him with the ball-peen hammer. Both. Either. One or the other. Cate didn't care, just long as he left her to own devices for a little while.

Another thing to add to her wish list. Something Cate knew she wouldn't get, given he hadn't moved anything except his mouth in almost three hours.

Grabbing the cage light, Cate hooked it to a different spot and turned her attention to the new filter she'd installed. She snapped the cap back on, then checked the radiator tube. The old one sat on the rolling tray alongside the rusty spark plugs. The one she'd replaced it with looked good. Solid brand name. Tight fit. Perfect for the big V-8. Screwdriver in hand, she tightened the clamp half a turn, then inspected her work.

Everything back in place and buttoned up tight.

The DieHard Gold battery she'd gotten from one of the cupboards at the back of the garage sat in its cradle, snug and secure, waiting to spark the engine she longed to hear turn over. Tugging on the cables, she checked the positive and negative connectors.

Yanking the rag out of her back pocket, she backed out from under the hood. Tired muscles complained. An ache set up shop between her shoulder blades. Setting the screwdriver on the fender pad, she stretched, attacking the strain.

"What next?" Dillinger asked.

"You keeping track of how many questions you asked tonight?" Wiping the grease from her hands with the stained scrap of cotton, Cate pivoted to face him. "How many was that—number five hundred?"

"You exaggerate."

"Not much of a stretch," she muttered, throwing him a dirty look.

His lips twitched. Again. For what seemed like the thousandth time.

About to boil over, Cate lowered the temperature on her temper. Maiming him would only add to her problems... and piss him off. And an angry Shadow Walker on top of worrying about Rannock was more than she could handle right now.

Tossing the rag onto the metal cart, she asked, "Got the keys?"

Dillinger blinked. "It's fixed?"

"Pretty much." She shrugged, acting nonchalant, feeing about ready to explode. Fingers crossed the Chevy cooperated and decided to turn over. The sooner she finished, the quicker Dillinger would keep his word and take the explosive out of her head. "A few minor adjustments, maybe, but she should run now."

"Seriously?"

"Yeah."

"For real?"

She scowled at him.

"Okay," he murmured, tone full skepticism. Here one second, gone the next. Eagerness pushed doubt out the way, lighting up his features. A weird shimmer entered his eyes. His I'm-too-cool-for-you slouch disappeared as his shoulder popped off the side of the column. He yanked the keys out of his pocket. "You wanna—"

"Your truck, your key to turn. Fire her up," she said, trying not to laugh at his expression. But man, it was hard. He looked like a kid at Christmas, all but dancing as he waited to find out what Santa had brought him during the night. "Let's see how she sparks."

Cloudflyer runners squeaking against polished concrete, Dillinger palmed the door handle. The lock popped. Freshly greased hinges opened on a soundless swing. A spring in his step, he hopped into the cab. She lost sight of him behind the raised hood, but heard him crank the window down. The ignition clicked. He hesitated, then turned the key.

The big V-8 caught.

A low growl filled the garage.

Dillinger laughed. "Brilliant, Cate! Absolutely brilliant."

She smiled, pleasure streaming through her. He said *brilliant*. She thought *perfect*. And it was. Absolute, pure, unadulterated happiness. No question about it. Nothing made satisfaction hum through her more than watching a beautiful, previously undrivable truck become road-worthy.

"Give it some gas," she yelled, watching the engine shimmy.

The smell of exhaust fumes in the air, Dillinger revved the engine.

Her eyes narrowed as she tilted her head and listened. Gorgeous snarl. Perfect timing. Just the right pitch. Clearing away the tools, cage light, and fender pads, she unhooked the lift bar and lowered the hood. Fingers holding the edge, she hesitated a second, then let the heavy piece of steel go.

The latch caught. The hood settled back into place. Dillinger grinned at her through the windshield.

Sharing his elation, she gave him two thumbs up. "You should take her for a drive."

He nodded, then cut the engine. Quiet returned to the garage. "I'll take it for a spin later. But first..."

Cate tensed as he opened the door and exited the cab.

Green eyes boring into hers, he flicked his wrist. The driver's-side door slammed closed. "A deal's a deal."

"Ah." Chewing on the inside of her cheek, Cate watched him approach. She backed up a step, then another. Her joy at getting the old truck running died a quick death. Unease replaced it as Dillinger rounded the front bumper. Cate retreated to the other side of the truck. She wanted the pod out of her head, no question, but...

All of a sudden, having Dillinger get close enough to touch her seemed like a terrible idea. One that might end with her in a coma. Or worse—dead.

Shuffling backward, Cate swallowed. "I think maybe we should wait for Rannock."

His brows popped skyward. "Don't trust me?"

"If you were me, would you trust you?"

He snorted.

"Seriously, Dillinger—would you?"

"Not gonna hurt you, woman," he said, deep voice full of impatience. Or hurt. She couldn't tell which. "We made a deal. The truck's running. You want the pod out of your head. Fair exchange, so just relax and—"

He jolted as his body seized. Air exited his lungs on a rasp. A second later, his knees hit the concrete floor.

Surprise tightened her chest. Cate froze beside the truck.

"Fuck," he growled as though in terrible pain. "The TriHexe. It's close, and I'm... I'm... Shit."

"What is it?" Watching him twitch, not knowing what to do, she took a step toward him. "What's wrong?"

Head bowed, one hand planted on the floor, the other quaking, he shook his head. "Cate, you need to... You've gotta—"

"What?"

"Get away from me."

A low snarl left his throat as he raised his head. Glowing green eyes collided with hers. His body contorted. Bones snapped. He groaned as he started changing into something monstrous. He looked like an enormous lion with gold-and-black fur... at first. But as he sprouted wings, then grew antlers and razor-sharp claws, Cate reconsidered. Dillinger wasn't turning into a lion, but an amalgamation of several different animals.

"Dillinger?"

The tip of the monster's tail swung around to face her. Fur morphed into scales as a huge snake head grew from the end.

On the floor, writhing in pain, Dillinger flashed blood-red fangs at her. "Run!"

Frozen in place, Cate flinched.

He roared at her again.

Her feet came unglued.

Boot soles sliding against smooth concrete, she lunged toward the rear of the truck, then sprinted behind a row of parked cars. Lungs pumping, she sped toward the stairs as her mind rejected the situation. Everything about it felt unreal. She was in a regular garage, surrounded by beautiful cars. Part of a normal, everyday scene. Nothing out of place—except for the Shadow Walker turning into a monster behind her.

Running flat out, she glanced back.

Slit eyes riveted to her, the snake hissed. Saliva dripped from long, needle-like fangs, splattering onto the floor.

Adrenaline hit her like rocket fuel.

Terror did the rest, propelling her around the last car in the row.

Heart hammering, arms and legs pumping, Cate focused on the stairs. She needed to make up the first flight, onto the landing, then around the corner where the stairwell narrowed. The tight stretch of staircase might buy her more time, the added seconds necessary for her to reach the upper hallway and scream for help.

She heard the creature's claw scrape across concrete and chanced another look back.

God help her. The monster was on its feet. Huge antlers swung around as it snapped its head toward her. The thing bared its fangs, unfolding black-and-gold wings.

A snarl rippled across the garage.

Air rasped against the back of her throat.

She wasn't going to make it. Forget about a future with Rannock. Never mind Scotland and building a new life far from the turmoil her father left in his wake.

As the monster took flight, Cate knew her fate was sealed. The certainty of it set. No more deals could be struck. Instinct told her the thing breathing down her neck wouldn't play let's-make-a-deal. Dillinger was gone, and she was about to be eaten alive.

21

Hearing the awful snarl and hiss behind her, Cate pushed herself to run faster. Her muscles quivered. Her lungs burned. Her mind rebelled as the monster chased her across the garage.

Huge wings flapped. A gust of air shoved her forward.

Panic and fear collided, amalgamating into pure terror as she stumbled mid-stride. Moving too fast to stop the momentum, she tucked her head and rolled into the fall. Luck pushed her into a full revolution, popping her back onto her feet. She kept moving, pumping her legs, using her arms to increase her speed.

Nothing but a lost cause.

Cate knew she was already dead. No way could she outrun the beast. The thing was too big. She might be running for her life, but it was nothing but a pipe dream.

She tried anyway, refusing to admit defeat. Her footfalls slammed against the smooth floor, propelling her toward the stairs. The one way out, her salvation if she made it that far. The landing acted like a beacon. She zeroed in, concentrating on reaching the steps and the hard left turn at the top that would take her up. The second she turned the corner, she'd be out of danger, at least for a minute or two, free to find a place to hide while Dillinger in monster form figured out how to follow her up the narrow stretch of staircase.

Heart hammering, eyes pinned to her target, she jetted between two columns. Time slowed down. Her body kept moving as the chaotic clamor inside her head quieted. Her thoughts crystalized. All the garbage in her life cleared out, leaving nothing but the important things behind.

Rannock, the Dragonkind warrior meant and made to be hers.

Nicole, the sister she loved more than classic cars and mechanics.

A new start in a foreign country full of people she'd never met, but already considered her family.

Running for her life did that to a girl—boiled things down, gave her perspective, sharpened instincts to a fine point while granting unwanted reality checks. Driving her to do better. *Be better*—kinder, smarter, more self-aware—before the universe wrote *The End* and closed the book on her life.

Funny how that happened.

In the moments before death, everything went still. The present became clearer. The past echoed louder. Every heartbeat yearned for the future, wishing and wanting as blood rushed in her veins and painful breaths rasped against the back of her throat. Each second she lived was a gift. Moments to be enjoyed, instead of endured.

Gratefulness streamed through her.

Seemed odd, but she *was* thankful. For lessons her father taught her, no matter how twisted. For the sister she loved. For having beaten the odds and found Rannock in a world where nothing came for free.

Not life. Not death.

And certainly not love.

Sprinting past a row of standing racks, Cate grabbed one. Full of discarded parts, the tall shelf tipped. Metal hit the ground with a crash. Boxes bounced off the floor. Tools pinwheeled over knotted cables as old car batteries went flying.

Less than ten feet behind her, Dillinger slammed into it, getting tangled up in the mess. Wings bent at odd angles, he ran into a pillar. Antlers clanged against concrete. Red fangs flashed as the monster howled. The snake tipping its tail snapped at the wires wound around his paws.

Seeking some cover, she zigzagged in behind another column, then ran flat out. She heard the monster flail. A battery whistled over her head. She ducked as more crap flew toward her. Momentum pushed her forward. Muscles burning with fatigue, she vaulted up the steps. Her toe caught a bad edge. She started to fall.

A huge paw swiped at her. Hooked claws nicked the back of her shirt.

"Rannock!" she screamed without knowing why. Her mate couldn't help her. Not now. Never again. He was miles away. She was alone and—

Sharp teeth clamped down on the back of her thigh.

Shock stole her breath. Pain gave it back.

Cate screamed again.

"Damn it, Dillinger," a voice growled from somewhere above her. "Let her go."

With a low snarl, the beast tightened its grip.

Clinging to the railing, she jerked.

"For fuck's sake, brother."

She recognized the voice. "Rathbone."

"Hold on, honey. Give me a sec..."

Tears blurring her eyes, she held on, curling her arms around the railing, hooking her elbows around the spokes. Movement flashed in her periphery. A sharp crack sounded. Bright blue light flashed behind her and—

Boom!

A bomb went off.

Wind whipped around her head. Car alarms went off. The pressure around her thigh eased. More flashes of light. Another crack ripped across the garage. With a whine, Dillinger let her go. Sharp teeth slid away from her skin.

Turning on the steps, she looked up into Rathbone's face. Blue eyes glowing, he grabbed the front of her shirt and threw her, one-handed, up the stairs. She landed with a thump on the landing. Rolling to a stop against the wall, she reached for the back of her leg, feeling for damage. Shredded denim. A few scrapes and scratches on her skin. No puncture wounds.

Eyes wide, she stared at Rathbone. Surrounded by a burning ball of electricity, he wielded a multi-tailed whip made of lightning. Electricity lashed the air. The fine hairs on her body stood on end as a shield appeared in his other hand. Her mouth dropped open as the whip swung overhead. He snapped his wrist. Strips of lightning flashed, driving Dillinger back across the garage. Supercharged current electrified the air.

Fury in his eyes, Rathbone glanced at her. "Move, Cate. Get out of here."

"Where?"

"Upper hallway. Get to the side entrance. Rannock needs you."

Numb inside and out, Cate pushed to her feet. Pain kicked. Holding the back of her bruised thigh, she obeyed and, with one last look at Rathbone, scrambled up the stairs on her hands and the balls of her feet.

Turning the corner, she raced the rest of the way up. Reaching the top in record time, she sped into the upper hall. She slid to stop, trying to orient herself. The side entrance. She must find the side entrance. Rathbone said Rannock needed her. She needed to—

A curse sounded a few feet away. "Jesus, Cate. What happened?"

Her gaze snapped to the right, landing on Noble. Heart racing, shock setting in, she stared at him in incomprehension.

Noble frowned. "Are you all right?"

She shook her head.

"What happened?"

"Dillinger attacked me."

"Lion with wings, antlers, and a viper tail?"

Cate nodded. "What was that thing?"

"One of Dillinger's forms."

Chest heaving, she threw him a wild look. "One of them?"

"The least cooperative one."

"Terrific," she said, doubling over, trying to catch her breath. Inhale. Exhale. Simple enough, but as her adrenaline drained, her hands started to shake. "Rathbone said… I need—"

"Rannock."

"Yeah." Swallowing past her sore throat, Cate pushed up from her knees. "Where's the side entrance?"

Noble pointed down the hall, in the opposite direction. "All the way down. Hook left at the dead end. I'll show you."

Alarm rang her internal bell. "Only if you promise not to turn into something weird."

His mouth curved. "Dillinger's got the market cornered on monsters. Rathbone and I are normal."

She doubted it.

Nothing about the Shadow Walkers approached anything normal.

With a quick pivot, Cate left Noble standing in the middle of the hallway and started for the side entrance. Favoring her bruised leg, she glanced over her shoulder. "He could've killed me. Could've had me by the throat—easy."

"He break any skin?"

Unable to stop herself, she ran her hand over the back of her jeans. Shredded in spots, ripped in others, holes the size of razor-sharp teeth. A shiver rolled through her. "A little. Nothing serious."

"Lucky he likes you, Cate."

"I don't feel lucky."

Noble chuckled.

"Not funny," she grumbled, reliving her terror-driven flight across the garage.

As recall shuddered through her, Cate upped her pace. She needed to see Rannock. Now. Before she lost all courage. After spending hours in a state of constant upheaval, she wanted his arms around her, and hers around him. To see his face, hear his voice, feel his warmth seep into her bones, sink deep down until her spirit settled and her heart rebounded.

Little things. Ones that made all the difference to a girl who liked routine.

Taking a shaky breath, she strode past a wide, spiraling staircase. The banister curled one way. She went the other. The wall angled to the left. The carpet followed, stopping at a dead end. Noble murmured behind her. The wall slid sideways, revealing a hidden passageway. Without missing a beat, Cate vaulted up the stone steps and, at the top, turned into a narrow corridor. Wood paneling funneled her into a large vestibule with antique floor tile. Feet planted in the middle of the chequerboard, she looked around.

A wooden door with wide side windows. An antique dresser pressed up against the back wall. Twin wall sconces aglow, throwing shadows across the coffered ceiling. Soft light. Ghosting quiet. Empty room.

Panic knocked on her emotional door.

She glanced at Noble. "Where is he?"

"Close."

"Noble—"

"Wait, sweetheart. Give him and the others a chance to land."

She wanted to argue. The urge to backtrack into mistrust banged around inside her head. Her temples started to ache, making her want to rant and rail. Fisting her hands, she pressed her fingernails into the palms. Sharp jabs of pain. Grounding pressure as the bite mark on her thigh started to throb. Trying to be patient, she ignored Noble and stared at the door, willing it to swing open, desperate for Rannock to—

A tingle swept across the nape of her neck.

The air around the door began to shimmer.

Gaze riveted to the entrance, Cate tensed as an archway appeared inside the door. Poised to take flight, she shifted to the balls of her feet. Heavy footfalls thumped. Fast rhythm. Hurried pace. A shadow fell across the threshold. A moment later, a huge blond man stepped inside.

Ice-blue eyes landed on her, then snapped to the Shadow Walker standing behind her. His upper lip curled. An instant later, he tossed a metal case at Noble.

He caught it.

"Bugger off, arsehole. Family only," the guy growled, exposing sharp canines. As Noble did as he was told, blue eyes came back to her. "Cate?"

"Yes," she said, throat so tight her voice cracked. "Who're you?"

"Levin." Smooth, deep, and rich, his Scottish brogue rolled toward her. "Ran's brother."

Fear rising, she searched the archway beyond Levin's shoulders. "Where's Ran? Where's my—"

"Lass," he said. "Donnae have a lot of time, so gonna say this quick. He's hurt. It's bad. Kruger and Tempel are bringing him in, and you need tae feed him."

Her stomach dipped. "How bad?"

"Worst I've ever seen. Without you, he willnae make it."

"I've never... How do I do that?" she said, beginning to shake.

"Feed him?"

Locking down the panic, Cate nodded, but reached into the back of her mind. Conversations with Nicole streamed into the breach. Her sister talked about feeding Vyroth all the time—and enjoyed every second—but she'd never explained the ins and outs of an energy exchange. Was it complicated? Would Rannock control everything? Or did she need to do something to ensure he got what he needed to heal?

"Tell me how, Levin."

"Strip down, lass. He needs you skin tae skin. Put your mouth on him, too. Tuck in tight, as close as you can get." Shifting out of the doorway, Levin sidestepped. "He'll connect. All you need do is accept."

"Okay." Flexing her fingers, she reached for the hem of her shirt.

"Listen well, Cate, 'cause it's important," he said, gaze drilling into hers. "You control the flow of energy. *You*, not him. Donnae let him take too much too quickly. He could kill you without meaning tae, steal your core energy... understood?"

"Yes," she said, whipping the shirt over her head.

Levin looked away. "I'll stay until the energy stream stabilizes. You need my help, lass, I'm here."

Toeing off her boots, Cate caught movement beyond the archway. Three guys crossed the threshold. Two under their own power. The other was unconscious, dark head bowed, tips of his boots dragging on the floor as the pair worked to bring him into the vestibule.

"Rannock," she whispered, unzipping her jeans.

Her mate twitched.

Tears pricking her eyes, she stripped down to nothing, uncaring who saw, and lunged toward him. His skin collided with hers. He snarled, a weak purr at the back of his throat. Doing as Levin instructed, Cate tucked in tight, pressing her mouth to his pulse point. Her hands landed on his back. Her breasts rested against his chest.

He arched, reacting as though she'd hit him with fifty thousand volts. Hard muscles flexed. Ice cold hands met her skin. Shock rippled through her. She jolted, but held the line, pulling him closer, fighting to keep him on his feet. Stumbling sideways, Rannock started to go down. His brothers steadied him, holding him upright as she burrowed in, praying the energy feeding started quickly.

Heat welled inside her. A click sounded inside her head. A burning sensation roared down her spine, making her tense against him. His mouth touched her temple. A flood of sensation whipped through her as she whispered to him, telling to take what he needed, that she loved him, asking him to stay with her.

Rannock groaned.

Cate quivered as the current picked her up and carried her along. Rushing her downstream. Making her senses sing and her skin tingle. Taking her to places she'd never been before.

Clinging to him, she ran her hand down his back, touching as much of him as she could reach. Cheek nestled against hers, he tightened his grip. She closed her eyes, allowing the rich stream to flow, giving everything she could, hoping she had what it took to give Rannock what he needed... and didn't lose her life in the process.

22

Muted whispers dragged Rannock out of the darkness. Odd echoes drifted, rippling through his head. Stilted words formed, then vanished, making him chase each one through the murk, through distant landscapes in his mind.

The murmur came again.

He tried to move. His body refused to respond, but sensory input trickled in, making him aware he hurt everywhere, from his scalp to the bottoms of his feet. Only one other thing registered through the haze of discomfort. Heat moved through his veins, the current so strong he turned toward the soothing wave. He let it wash over him, leaning into the stream until a seam opened in the ebb and flow, allowing a sliver of light into the gloom.

His muscles twitched, jerking as the warm connection continued knitting the two halves of him into a whole. A slow process. A gentle weave. Little by little, he sank back into his own body. Though...

Rannock frowned.

He couldn't feel anything. Not really. He knew all his limbs were attached, could sense the truth of his fingertips, but nothing else registered. He was numb, inside and out, on overload or something. Fighting to regain his senses, he clung to the heat, drifting in the stream. Wave after wave rolled in. Advance and retreat. Over and over. Again and again.

A sense of something came to him. Enthralling heat settled along his left side. Comfort in the press of soft skin. Powerful bio-energy encircled him, creating a protective cocoon, insulating him from the outside world.

Swallowing past his sore throat, he tucked in, getting closer, needing more. More of the heat warming him. More of the stream feeding him. More of the delicious taste in his mouth.

Words came and went.

He drifted in the current, bathing in a river of sensation as it dragged him upstream. So good. The place he inhabited was phenomenal. Warm. Soft. Beautiful. Unlike anything he knew. Better than everything he'd experienced.

The realization moved him closer to comprehension.

Fighting through the murk, Rannock battled to catch hold of a thought. Airy and uncooperative, each one swirled past. The current increased, feeding him more, helping him break the surface. The mental blur began to clear. Bit by bit, the pace increased. He groaned. Delicious taste on his tongue. Gorgeous energy in his veins. Dead to the world, lost for hours, his dragon half stirred deep inside him.

Emotion swelled.

His throat tightened.

"*There you are,*" he thought at his beast, feeling the two halves of his whole reconnect.

Thank the goddess. He was still alive.

He remembered the tear—the slicing agony as his dragon half turned away, ripping him in two. A brutal sensation; a terrifying occurrence. He'd never been separated from his better half before. The beast was always just *there*, lurking deep inside him, faithful, lethal, ready to be called upon at a moment's notice. Not once in almost two hundred years had he doubted his ability to shift and become what he was meant to be—a Dragonkind warrior few, if any, ever challenged.

Turning inward, Rannock embraced the claw and hiss. His dragon half woke a little more. He drew it closer. Tears pricked the backs of his eyes. *"There you are, you ornery bastard."*

In a pissy mood, his beast bared his fangs.

Gladness filled him as he dove deeper, reveling in the powerful energy infusing his muscles, sinking into his bones, feeding his soul. Mental acuity sparked, becoming clearer. Imperfect perception. Nowhere close to normal, but tracking better, his situational awareness sharpened.

He was inside, out of the wind. Lying on something soft. Blankets, maybe. A bed, perhaps.

Unable to open his eyes yet, he hunted for more information. Quiet drifted as he sank back into full sensation. The pain moved from harsh to lingering. Tingling fingers and toes. Bare skin against his. Soft hair in his face. A small hand pressed to the center of his chest. The scent of strawberries and lime combined with the smell of motor oil. Or maybe it was grease combined with scent of exhaust fumes.

Still groggy, he swallowed, working moisture back into his mouth. What he was feeling didn't make sense. He couldn't puzzle out what—

Indistinct whispers solidified into words.

"He's coming around," someone said.

"Thank fuck. How's Cate?"

Covers rustled. The surface he lay on shifted.

Eyes closed, unable to find his voice, he bared his teeth in warning.

"Not gonna touch her, lad," a male said. "Just assessing."

His brow furrowed. He tried to shake his head. Nothing moved.

"How is she?" a third voice asked, entering his mental sphere.

"Sleeping now, but holding it together."

"Good. Strong female." Muffled footfalls shuffled as males shifted around him. Rannock narrowed his focus. Soft surface with short fibers. An area rug, maybe. "And his dragon?"

Arctic chill spilled over him. A second later, a cool hand cupped the side of his neck. "Back from the brink."

"Jesus." Someone exhaled, sounding relieved. "That was close."

"Too close. I'm going tae take a chunk out of Rathbone."

A low growl sounded in agreement. "Burn his fucking house to the ground."

The threat rode on an American accent.

"Me first," Rannock rasped, finding his voice.

Someone chuckled.

Body beginning to cooperate, he cracked his eyes open.

An ice-blue gaze met his. Levin smiled. "There you are. Welcome back, Ran."

"Cate."

"She's good, brother. Tucked up tight against you," Levin said, releasing his hold on him. "Feel her?"

Rannock's fingers flexed as he forced his arm to move. An insignificant twitch, hardly any movement at all, but enough for him to feel his female against his side. His chest went tight. He breathed out in relief. "You sure?"

"Aye, lad. She's okay. Feeding you well… lots of powerful energy." Bumping Levin with his shoulder, Kruger came into view. "She's a champ, Ran."

"Lucky bastard," Tempel said, setting up shop at the foot of the bed.

Battling to stay awake, Rannock swallowed past his sore throat. "Update."

"We're at Habersham House until you're fit tae travel," Levin said.

"Emerald Room?" he asked, unable to focus on anything but his brothers-in-arm's faces. Though at least now the mattress beneath his back registered. The warm weight of Cate along his side, beneath the covers with him, too. He relaxed into the sensation, loving her softness, absorbing the perfection of her bio-energy as it brought him back to life. "Her sire?"

"Caged until Rathbone figures out what tae do with him, but…"

As Levin trailed off, Rannock exhaled. "He isnae going tae make it. Too far gone."

Kruger nodded. "He's in a bad way, brother."

"Fuck," he murmured, concern for his mate rising. Henry Biscayne—total fucking screw-up. Not that the truth would help his mate. Cate loved her sire. Losing him would wound her. Given a chance, Rannock would've shielded her, stepped between her and the pain. Gathered her up, wrapped her in cotton batting, and kept the woes of the world from her doorstep. Some things, however, couldn't be hidden… or avoided. He clenched his teeth. His female needed to know the truth, would want to say goodbye before the end came. "That's gonna hurt."

A round of "*ayes*" bounced around the room.

Silence spilled in the wake of resounding agreement.

The sound of a fire crackled, breaking up the quiet, lulling him toward relaxation.

"I'm just gonna..."

"Sleep, Ran. Nothing needs doing now." Stepping away from the bed, Levin flipped the covers back up.

Eyes drifting closed, Rannock shifted beneath the sheets and, turning on his side, curled into Cate. Her warmth welcomed him. Her energy nourished him. The beauty of her soothed him in ways he didn't comprehend. Then again, he no longer needed to—not with the bond between him and his female in full effect.

Energy-fuse in all its glory.

A wonder to behold.

Murmuring her name, Rannock wrapped both arms around her. He caressed the back of her thigh and hooked her knee over his hip. Face nestled against her throat, he settled in. She sighed, pressing close, making room for him as his packmates moved away from the bed.

He heard the quiet creak as two males settled in chairs near the hearth. A door clicked as another left the room.

Body exhausted, but mind working better now, Rannock started compiling a to-do list. First and foremost—thank his mate the second she woke up. She'd saved his life, dragging him away from certain death. Without her, he'd be nothing but dragon ash drifting on a night breeze. In a foreign country, a place he couldn't wait to leave.

He wanted to go home. Needed to introduce Cate to the rest of his pack and get her settled into her new life. One they would spend a lifetime building together.

Lovely thoughts. All worthy of his time and attention.

Too bad none of it had any chance of happening until he managed to haul his arse out of bed. The second Rannock regained his strength, Rathbone and his kin were in for a nasty surprise. One that included his fist in their faces and lots of broken bones. After that, he'd deal with Cate's sire, do what he could to soften the blow and lessen her pain.

An impossible task.

Mourning a loved one was never easy. Missing one never went away. No one knew that better than him.

23

Sun warm on her skin, Cate lay in a cocoon of endless comfort. Images flashed across her mind. Piercing blue water. A long stretch of golden beach. Palm trees above her head. Cushioned lounger at her back. Paradise with unending supplies of iced glasses full of fruit-flavored drinks. Perfect with just the right amount of punch.

A hot breeze drifted over her. Gentle strokes. Heated swirls. Light mist landed on her belly, feathered over her breasts, and drifted over her thighs.

Relaxed beneath the soothing rise and fall, she sighed. Such a pretty place. Picture perfect. Full of sun, fun, and the wash of gentle waves. A spot without barriers as she lay naked beneath the noonday sun.

The breeze drifted over her again. Her skin came alive. Her body warmed even more. Lifting her arms over her head, she arched into the sensation and—

A pulsing wave of pleasure throbbed through her. As bliss crested, her tropical cocoon tore open. She rocketed from fast asleep to somewhat awake and mostly confused. Struggling to get her bearings, she twisted as another blistering wave rolled through her.

Her back arched. Her eyes popped open and—

"What?" she mumbled, looking down her body.

Naked in the middle of a big bed. Knees spread wide. Rannock, big hands holding her hips, with his dark head buried between her thighs. Hazel-orange eyes met hers over the mound of her sex. She rasped his name. He licked over her clit, bathing her in heat, killing her with pleasure.

"Shit," she gasped, reaching down to fist her hand in his hair.

He laughed.

The vibration tweaked sensitive nerve endings. Her core throbbed. She whimpered a second before he drew her into his mouth. Hot breath. Gentle suction. A tease. A taunt. With a curse, she arched. As the back of her head pressed into the sheets, she raised her hips, begging him for more. Lashing her with his tongue, he gave her what she wanted. More pressure. Blistering heat. Beautiful intensity.

"Ran…"

He stroked over her again, using the flat of his tongue.

"Ran!"

With a growl, he sucked… hard.

And she went off like a bomb, coming so hard he dragged a scream from the back of her throat.

"Beautiful, lass. Go again."

Chest heaving, body pulsing, Cate snarled at him. "Make me."

He smiled against her.

Spreading her wider, he licked deeper. The sharp edge of his teeth grazed her. Her knees jerked as she moaned. Holding her down, he added two fingers and thrust deep. Zero hesitation. No mercy. Nothing but ecstasy as he found a sensitive spot deep inside her. Working her hard, he drove her higher. Inch by inch.

Over tsunamis of cresting waves, finding new territory, making her twist beneath him.

Out of breath, desperate with need, she begged without words.

He eased the pressure. "Tell me, Cate."

She moaned in protest.

Backing off even more, he kissed the inside of her thigh. "You know what I want tae hear."

She shook her head.

"Give it tae me."

"Please."

"Good, *Bellmia*... and?"

"I..."

"What?"

"Love you," she rasped, struggling to breathe.

"Aye, Catie-mine, you do." Using the tip of his tongue, he circled her clit. One rotation turned into two, then more, keeping her on edge, driving her wild, making her writhe beneath him. "I love you too, and now, you're gonna come for me again. This time, though, you're gonna say my name when you do."

Another gentle lick.

Head tipped back, Cate shuddered.

"You gonna say my name, *Bellmia*?"

"Yes."

"Aye, you are," he growled, settling back in, giving her what she needed while she gave him what he asked, coming hard, doing it calling his name.

"Gorgeous," he murmured, shifting between her thighs. Notched against her, he pushed deep, filling her full. "Fuck, but you're good. Unbelievably sweet."

"Ran," she whispered, wrapping her arms and legs around him.

"Been waiting so long, lass. So bloody long for you."

One orgasm rolled into another. With a gasp, Cate clenched around him.

He groaned and started to move, giving her his weight as she gave him her mouth. Hands buried in his hair, she tangled her tongue with his, needing his taste in her mouth, enthralled by the beauty of him. Kissing her back, he rode her gently, rocking deep, retreating slow, sharing his love without words, allowing her to feel every inch of him—mind, body, heart, and soul.

Trailing her fingers down his back, she broke the kiss.

His eyes opened.

"Rannock," she said, holding his gaze as he moved inside her.

His breathing hitched. The orange in his hazel eyes started to shimmer. "Catie-mine."

Cate raised her head and brushed his mouth with hers. "I am yours. Do you doubt it?"

"Nay."

"You sure?"

"Aye."

"Good," she whispered, rolling her hips, meeting his deepening thrusts.

"Goddess," he said, heart thundering, voice rumbling. "I'm close, baby... so close."

"Take me rough. Take me gentle. Take me any way you want, Ran."

"My mate." Upping the pace, he hammered her with powerful stokes. "So beautiful."

Gaze riveted to his face, she met and matched him, watching pleasure overtake him. Lips parted, head thrown back, he shook in her arms. Memorizing every nuance, Cate held on tight as he careened over the edge, throbbing deep inside her.

Unable to hold himself up, Rannock folded forward, relaxing into her. Taut muscles went lax. His body grew heavy against hers as he nestled his face in her throat.

Skin to skin, as close as two people could get, Cate wrapped him up. Closing her eyes, she pressed her cheek against his temple. His scent enveloped her, surrounding her with spice and sandalwood. Decadent. Delicious. One hundred percent Rannock.

She murmured to him. Incoherent things. Precious little nothings. Secrets of the heart. The language of love. One she hadn't learned and never would have if not for Rannock.

Her dragon. Generous beyond measure.

The way he treated her humbled her. The way he loved her made her glad to be the woman he'd chosen to mate. She liked everything about him—the edge he wore like armor, the sense of humor he hid strong feelings behind, how open-hearted he became when he knew he was loved.

Her throat went tight.

A month with him in her life, most of it spent on the phone… that was all. Barely any time at all. And yet he'd become so important to her Cate wondered how she'd ever survived without him.

Overwhelmed, she cupped the nape of his neck and whispered, "Thank you."

He stirred. "Think that's my line, lass."

"Probably."

His mouth curved against the side of her throat.

Winding thick strands around her fingertips, she played with the curling ends of his hair. "Ran?"

"Aye?"

"Are you okay?"

"Just loved you hard, Catie-mine. You really need tae ask?"

"You were hurt."

"Not anymore," he said, lifting his head. Warm eyes met hers as he planted one forearm on the mattress and raised his other hand. His palm settled against her cheek. Watching his fingers move across her skin, he stroked over her bottom lip with his thumb. "Got what I needed. What I'll always need. She's lying right here with me."

A compliment. Big, bold, and beautiful. Bright and shiny emotion in his eyes. No attempt to hide how he felt about her.

Pleasure shivered through her.

He traced her lips with his fingertip.

She nipped him, teeth grazing his skin. "I was worried. Are you sure you're—"

"Fully recovered, lass," he said, holding her gaze. "Won't lie, I was in a bad way when I first woke up. Verra shaky, but now, I feel good. Normal. No lasting weakness. The last few hours with you wiped it away."

She breathed out in relief. "I had no idea what I was doing. Whether you were getting enough."

"Got more than enough. Seriously, *Bellmia*. No need for you tae worry."

She nodded, relaxing into his reassurance.

"I wanna make love tae you again." Still inside her, Rannock pressed his hips into hers. Sensitive places quivered. She drew in a quick breath through her nose. Dipping his head, he kissed her. Once. Twice. A third time. Soft touches. Butterfly brushes. Lovely little sips. "But it's already late afternoon."

"So?"

"We need tae get up. Shower. Get dressed."

"I don't like that plan."

He chuckled. "Me either, but my brothers are waiting, and we need tae talk before the impatient bastards storm in here."

She blinked. *Talk?*

Her stomach clenched as her mood shifted from playful to serious. Rannock wasn't joking. She saw it on his face. When he said talk, what he really meant was *talk!* Which all pointed to an issue so big he would've preferred to ignore it, but out of deference to her, refused to avoid.

"How much am I going to dislike this talk?"

"On a scale of one to ten?"

She nodded.

"Five thousand and fifty-seven."

"Shit," she whispered, closing her eyes.

"Cate, look at me."

Drawing a fortifying breath, she did as he asked. The concern in his eyes cranked her even tighter. She wanted to look away, ignore his pain on her behalf, shove her rising suspicions away, but...

She'd never been big on denial.

The truth mattered. A lifetime spent living with a liar had taught her a few things. She faced challenges, instead of allowing others to fight battles for her. She managed the chaos and absorbed the pain. Sad to say, but somewhere along the line, minimizing the damage had become her specialty. Countless lessons over too many years informed the way she moved through the world, ensuring she never buried her head in the sand.

Like a Band-Aid. Rip it off like a Band-Aid.

Her motto. The hard and fast rule she lived by never steered her wrong.

Stroking her hair, Ran murmured, "Catie-mine."

"It's about my dad, isn't it?"

He sighed. "*Bellmia*, I wish I had better news, but it isnae good. He's—"

A knock sounded on the door.

With a growl, Rannock rolled across the mattress. Arms around her, he took her with him, tumbling toward the edge of the bed. His feet hit the floor. Tangled up in the sheet, Cate landed beside him. Shock thumped through her as she stared up at his stormy expression.

"Who is it?"

"Rathbone," he said, a violent undercurrent in his tone.

A second rap, sharper than the first, rolled into the room.

Eyes narrowed on the door, Rannock muttered something. The temperature in the room dropped. Embers in the hearth flared as the air warped around him, exploding into metallic shimmer and...

Presto.

Wave a magic wand.

Jeans and a long-sleeved Henley appeared on his muscular frame. Boots settled on his feet. "Get dressed, lass."

"Ah." Shocked by his get-dressed-with-a-murmur magic, she stared at him a second. A muscle in his jaw twitched. She got with the program and, biting her lower lip, looked down at the sheet pressed to her chest, then around Emerald Room. Same pretty wallpaper. Same fourposter bed. Same armchairs in front of the fireplace. Neither of which held any of her clothes. "I left them in the vestibule."

His dark brows popped toward his forehead.

"Long story," she said, unwilling to go into details with Rathbone banging on the door. "Maybe—"

"Here," he said, handing her something.

She grabbed the bundle without looking. Soft material settled in her hands. Surprised, she glanced down at a pair of black jeans and an oversized, periwinkle-blue cashmere sweater. A pair of ankle boots with wide side zippers and chunky wooden heels landed beside her feet. Expensive name brands. Designer gear. Pretty in a slouchy, I'm-a-trendy-girl-about-town kind of way.

Words escaped her.

Rannock kissed the top of her head. With a quick pivot, he left her battling shock beside the bed and prowled toward the door. Cate watched him a moment, then dropped the sheet and yanked the sweater over her head. She tackled the jeans next, doing a dance, wiggling into stretchy black denim, then grabbed one of the boots. Going commando beneath her clothes wasn't ideal. Some underwear in the whole conjuring-of-stylish-clothes thing would've been nice, but...

Whatever. No time for splitting hairs. She needed to hurry. The way Rannock moved spoke volumes.

None of it good.

The second her dragon opened the door, the Shadow Walker standing on the other side was in for a surprise. A nasty one that would include a face full of pissed-off dragon warrior and lots of bloodshed.

24

Striding around the end of the fourposter bed, Rannock battled the need to level the male standing outside in the corridor. Magic sparked in his veins. He made some quick calculations. A lethal strike of magnetic force. Bronze combined with gleaming steal edges. Knives blasting through the heavy wood of the bedroom door... straight into Rathbone's chest.

Wouldn't take much.

The work of seconds.

A soft command.

The flick of his fingertips, and he'd launch an arsenal, lay waste to the Shadow Walker testing his patience. Burn Habersham House to the ground. Never have to deal with the bastard again.

A nice thought. One his vicious nature urged him to make manifest.

Tightening the grip on his temper, Rannock slowed his pace instead. His boots thumped across thick carpet. He rolled his shoulders, took a deep breath, and reached for control. Not an easy feat, given his current need to annihilate. Rathbone interrupting his time with Cate was one thing. The pod the bastard had placed at the base of her skull was quite another.

The fact the implant remained active pissed him off. He'd done as Rathbone demanded and retrieved the TriHexe. The instant he realized Rannock approached Habersham House carrying the magical device, Cate should've been freed, allowed to leave the house, meet him and his brothers outside on the street, instead of remaining trapped inside.

Rathbone should've kept his word. Immediately. An honorable male would've moved to ensure the safety of a female in his care, instead of endangering Cate much longer than necessary.

The realization cranked him tighter, which made his need to rip the male's head off much more difficult to ignore.

Not that he would act on it. Not yet.

Cate remained in danger until the pod was removed. Sucked for him, but he must abide by Rathbone's rules. Stay calm. Play the game the Shadow Walker's way—for now.

The second he eliminated the threat to his mate, however, the conversation—and his approach—would change in ways Rathbone and his brothers wouldn't appreciate. A dangerous endeavor, given the magic the male commanded.

Rannock didn't care.

A lesson needed to be taught. The bastard must be made to understand involving innocent humans (females in particular) in the games he played wouldn't be tolerated. Not by him. Not by his brothers-in-arms or any Dragonkind who sided with the Scottish pack.

Distance meant nothing. The miles between Savannah and Scotland could be navigated. Spies could be sent. With a little incentive, and a lot of money,

Dragonkind warriors who'd approached the Scottish pack looking for a new home could be convinced to relocate. Tabs could be kept on the trio of Shadow Walkers without difficulty, ensuring the brothers stayed on the straight and narrow.

The possibilities were endless.

The best one, however, rested closer to Georgia. He'd picked up the scent upon arrival, detected the whiff of magic in the air and knew what it meant. Another Dragonkind pack moved through the area on a regular basis. The unique energy signature wasn't difficult to follow.

Magic moved in the wind along the coastline. Slight vibrations. Telltale signs. Trace energy in the ocean currents. All indications a good-sized pack called the Eastern Seaboard home. Where, precisely? Somewhere close by his kind's standards. No farther than a thousand miles away. Easy flying distance for a Dragonkind fighting triangle.

Interesting discovery on his part.

Especially if he made contact.

Having an ally on the East Coast of the United States might solve his problem. He suspected Rathbone hadn't told him the whole story. Now, Rannock knew for sure. After handling the TriHexe, he understood its power. Raw. Elemental. Full of killing magic. He'd barely been able to contain it, even in a carrying case. His dragon half had suffered. He'd been come close to death, which meant...

Henry Biscayne hadn't stolen it. Not from inside Habersham House. Not from outside it, either. The TriHexe was simply too powerful for a human to hold, so...

Only one conclusion to draw.

Rathbone had hired Henry to do a job. He'd enlisted the human male's services for a reason, to further his cause and achieve a specific goal—before the plan went to shite, forcing the Shadow Walkers to improvise by kidnapping Cate.

As far as theories went, Rannock's was a good one. No way to corroborate it, though. Rathbone was a secretive bastard. He would never reveal his true plan to a pack of dragon warriors capable of stopping him.

The circular argument led Rannock back to the beginning—the mystery pack who'd set down roots within striking distance of Savannah. With allied Dragonkind warriors scouting, he wouldn't need to worry about Rathbone. He'd have eyes on the trio, be able to assess from afar as well as build a strong alliance with others of his kind.

An intriguing idea, though dragging the mystery pack out of the shadows might prove to be a problem. The fact no one knew the group existed spoke volumes. Whoever commanded the pack wanted to stay hidden, had no intention of joining the wider Dragonkind community.

A good plan, as far as strategies went.

Rannock knew it firsthand. After the murder of his uncle, Cyprus had closed their borders fifty years ago, shutting down all communication with the outside world. Other packs continued to reach out... at first. When his commander refused to engage—killing any warrior stupid enough to cross into territory protected by him and his brothers-in-arms—other commanders quit trying.

Radio silence.

Needed at the time.

But more difficult as the years wore on.

The trauma might've strengthened his pack, bringing them closer together, but isolation took its toll. Loss of reputation was the least of it. The lack of community hurt more. But after Rodin's (leader of the Archguard) treachery, everyone outside the Scottish pack became suspect. No one could be trusted. Cyprus had been right to retreat, but being mated changed a male's perspective. The instant Cyprus met Elise, things shifted. Now, he wanted allies, strong warriors in positions of power all over the global to combat the Archguard and the slow erosion of Dragonkind principles.

The idea of alliances was in its infancy, but grew by the day. After half a century of isolation, bridges between the Scottish pack and others were being built. The Nightfuries in Seattle were on board. A meeting between Cyprus and Bastian was already in the works, which gave him hope.

Hope for a better future. Hope for the continued good health of his kind. Hope that the power-mongering in Prague, seat of the Archguard and Dragonkind elite, could be stopped. That the coming battle could be fought and won.

Lofty ideals. A difficult goal.

Getting commanders from different parts of the world to agree wouldn't be easy. But convincing a pack that preferred to fly under the radar to join the cause would prove even more difficult. The risk, however, was worth the reward. A commander followed by strong warriors with no ties to the Archguard—or loyalty to Rodin—would be a valuable asset in the fast-approaching war. Now, and in the future.

Which meant he needed to call home and update his commander. Sooner, rather than later. Cyprus would want to know about—

A sharp knock rattled the brass knob.

Feet planted six feet from the door, Rannock swallowed a growl and flicked his fingers. The antique key sticking out of the lock flipped sideways. The click echoed inside his head a moment before he murmured a command. Well-oiled hinges hissed as the wooden panel swung open.

Shimmering blue eyes collided with his.

"I want it taken out," he said, refusing to be polite. He didn't care where he stood—inside the Shadow Walker's home, under his roof. Courtesy belonged to males who respected boundaries, not those who implanted explosive devices inside a female's head. "Now."

"Why I'm here, Rannock," Rathbone murmured, stepping over the threshold. "You kept your end of the bargain, I'll keep mine."

Blocking the bastard's path to Cate, Rannock flexed his hands. "Could've taken it out sooner, Rathbone. The second you knew I had the—"

"And touch your mate without your permission?" Rathbone raised a brow. "I've never lacked courage, dragon, but one thing I don't have is a death wish."

Temper frothing, Rannock's eyes started to glow. Orange-bronze shimmer washed over the male standing within striking distance.

Rathbone shifted, but held his ground, refusing to back down.

He drew a deep breath, clinging to control, 'cause... shite. The bastard had a point. Rannock might've suspected Cate was his mate, but he hadn't known for sure until he saw and touched her for the first time. No one could've guessed the depth of his connection to her. Not even Rathbone when he inserted the pod inside her head. And yet...

Rannock wanted to hold a grudge. He played nice instead, needing the Shadow Walker to keep his word

—for Cate to be safe—before he rearranged the arsehole's face. "I'll grant you that."

Rathbone's mouth twitched. "Big of you."

His eyes narrowed. "Take it out."

"Of course." The Shadow Walker looked past him to where Cate stood.

Rannock sensed her stiffen behind him. Refusing to take his eyes off the target, he held out his hand, palm up, without looking at her. "Settle, *Bellmia*. I willnae allow any harm tae come tae you."

"I know," she said, sounding confident when he knew she wasn't.

His mate was more than uncertain. She was tense, unsure of Rathbone, aware of Rannock's need to do violence. His mate—so bloody smart. She read him well, tuning into his moods, understanding his nature, accepting his needs. No matter how violent his tendencies.

Holding steady, he kept his hand out and waited, inviting her to come to him, refusing to rush her.

Her boot soles twisted against the carpet. A slight hesitation in her steps, then...

Light footfalls tapped across the floor as she approached his back. Her scent reached him. Awareness of her, always close to his surface, bloomed. Warm sensation prickled down his spine as she settled against him. Using his body as cover, Cate set her hands against his back and pressed her forehead between his shoulder blades.

He widened his stance, shielding her completely.

She nestled in, seeking his warmth, taking solace in the closeness, drawing on his strength. He gave it without thought. Reaching out with his mind, he linked in, then sank into the flow. Looping the current connecting him to her, he sent a wave of soothing energy to her, calming her, steadying himself, allowing her to hide behind him as long as she wanted.

The stalemate between him and Rathbone stretched.

Dying embers in the fireplace popped.

Cate drew a long breath, then let go, slipping out from behind him. Her small hand slid into his much larger one. Dark blue eyes met his. "I don't like the idea of him touching me, Ran."

He murmured in understanding.

Rathbone made a rough sound. "Won't take long, Cate. Thirty seconds, tops."

Her brow furrowed. "You shouldn't have put it inside my head in the first place."

"Desperate measures—"

"Makes a woman want to beat the shit out of Shadow Walkers."

With a huff, Rannock wound his arm around her.

Rathbone chuckled.

Cate scowled. "Seriously, Rathbone. No matter what my dad did, you messing with me is screwed up. I don't care how powerful you are, or how pissed off it makes you. I'm saying this for the next girl unfortunate enough to cross your path—please stop doing this kind of crap."

"Your objection is noted."

"I want it on the record."

Rathbone's gaze left her and landed on him. "She's fierce."

"Believe it," Rannock said with a nod.

"Lucky male."

"Believe that too."

Rolling her eyes, Cate threw a perturbed look at Rathbone. "I haven't heard you promise."

Pale eyes sparkling with amusement, the Shadow Walker tipped his chin. "You've my word, Cate."

"Good," she whispered, fingers twitching against Rannock's.

He squeezed her hand. "Ready?"

"No."

A chuckle escaped him. Completely inappropriate, but hell, he couldn't help it. The blunt edge of her honesty always surprised—and never failed to amuse him.

He gave her another squeeze. "*Bellmia*—"

"All right." A death grip on his hand, she glanced up at him. He nodded. She nodded back. "But you keep a hold of me the whole time."

"I will."

"The *whole* time, Ran."

"I willnae let you go, lass."

"Okay," she said, glancing at Rathbone. "Let's get it over with."

Flexing his hands, Rathbone pressed his chin to his chest. He rolled his neck, then his shoulders. His irises went from pale blue to shimmering gold. He tipped his chin.

Releasing her hand, Rannock turned her to face him, away from Rathbone, and drew her deeper into his arms. "Forehead pressed to my chest, Cate. Keep your chin tipped down. Stay as still as you can, aye?"

Her lashes flickered as she shut her eyes and nestled in, pressing her forehead to the center of his chest. "Don't let go."

"Got you," he said, hands flat against her spine, one between her shoulder blades, the other pressed to her lower back.

Gaze aglow, Rathbone stepped behind her. Electricity sparked in the air. Blue light radiated, pulsing through the room. He raised his hands.

Rannock tightened his hold. "Breathe, lass."

She inhaled long and slow.

Moving closer, the Shadow Walker made contact.

Cate flinched.

Murmuring reassurances, Rannock held her steady as Rathbone's hands settled on her. Middle fingers pressed to her temples, he placed his thumbs at the base of her skull. Cate tightened her grip on Rannock. His stomach clenched as powerful magic surged around her, then prickled through him. Static crawled across his skin, making Cate's short blond hair stand on end.

"Ouch," she said through clenched teeth.

Feeling her discomfort, Rannock growled.

"Hold tight," Rathbone muttered, circling his thumbs. "Almost there."

Lightning spun into a web around the Shadow Walker. A blue ball formed, creating a barrier between him and the rest of the room. Rathbone murmured in a foreign language, evoking the power of an ancient tongue. Cate started to shiver. A pod the size of a small seed flew from the base of her skull. Glowing bright, the implant hovered in midair a moment.

The electrified ball contracted around the explosive.

Letting go of Cate, Rathbone turned his hand.

Contained inside the orb, the pod settled in the center of the Shadow Walker's palm. A pop sounded. Bright light exploded inside the sphere. Rathbone breathed out. The glow in his gaze faded as he looked at Rannock. "Done."

"You sure?"

He nodded.

"You've left nothing behind?"

"Not a speck," Rathbone said, releasing a pent-up breath. "She's clear. No lasting harm."

Dipping his head, Rannock set his mouth to her temple and cupped the back of her head. His dragon half rose. Magic moved through his veins as he scanned her skull, looking for the lie, making sure Rathbone spoke true.

No blip on his radar. No foreign material embedded inside her brain. Nothing but a whole lot of normal.

Relief slammed through him. He closed his eyes and, hugging her a wee bit tighter, asked, "Feel all right?"

A slight shift in his arms as she assessed. "The low-grade headache that's been bugging me is gone, so... yeah. I think so."

"Good, lass."

She shivered against him. "Can we talk about my dad now?"

"In a minute." Opening his eyes, he stared at Rathbone from beneath his brows.

The male jerked in surprise, then began to back away.

Baring his teeth, Rannock picked Cate up and set her behind him. One moment, he stood in front of his mate. The next, he went after Rathbone.

Cate sucked in a quick breath. A second later, she yelled his name.

Too little to deter him. Too late to stop him.

He already had Rathbone by the throat. Picking him up, he tossed him through the open doorway into the corridor. The bastard needed a lesson, one Rannock looked forward to delivering... with his fists.

25

Thrown off his feet, Rathbone reeled backward. Green-and-gold wallpaper whirled in the periphery. He saw the doorjamb an instant before he collided with it. Wood bit into the back of his shoulder. Knocked off balance, he careened into the corridor. His shoes rasped across wooden floor, then slid onto carpet.

Struggling to get his feet under him, he wheeled his arms. A great strategy. Not that it mattered. He was off balance, too out of control to stop the inevitable or avoid the pain.

With a grunt, he slammed into the wall opposite Emerald Room. His shoulders punched through paint and gyprock. Plaster dust flew. The wide, rigid chair rail hammered his lower back. As agony clawed up his spine, a male consumed by righteous anger strode over the threshold.

Magic exploded down the corridor.

The wave liquified, splashing like black paint across the large window at the end of the hall, blocking out late-afternoon sunlight. As darkness descended, programmed wall sconces flickered, starting to come on.

Rathbone bared his teeth.

Rannock snarled back, slamming the bedroom door closed behind him.

Good call.

Cate Biscayne might be fierce, but she didn't need to witness the fight. Battles between magic wielders always ended in bloodshed, lots of it, and humans—no matter the affiliation with his kind—had no place ringside when immortals settled disagreements in the old way. The most natural way. By locking horns and using fists to communicate displeasure.

Though, to be fair, after what he'd done, she had every right to watch Rannock avenge her.

Rathbone wanted to object, disagree with the verdict and defend his actions. Problem was, he couldn't. Not really. He might've done what he believed necessary, but the best thing wasn't always the right thing. Sometimes right equaled wrong. Sometimes a male needed to make decisions that hurt others to achieve greater goals. Critical ones to ensure the health of all, even if it meant sacrificing one. Still...

As much as it pained him, he couldn't disagree with Rannock's position. Particularly since he understood what drove the male—righteous indignation brought on by fear for his mate and the need to protect her. At all costs. Even death, which Rannock courted by challenging him. Then again, Rathbone courted the same by accepting a fight with an enraged dragon warrior.

Dragonkind warriors weren't lightweights. The breed was vicious in and out of dragon form, more than capable of doing damage to Rathbone and his brothers. All the more reason to keep from tweaking a dragon's tail if it could be avoided.

Here, however? Avoidance was futile.

Rannock had something to prove. The need to assert his dominance was part of the equation. The greater share, however, belonged to rage. The purity of it shocked Rathbone, making him realize something important. He deserved Rannock's wrath. Every bit of it. If he had a mate, and she'd been threatened, he'd be reacting the same way, with unmeasured violence in order to make a point. Do it loud. Do it fast. Do as much damage as possible, ensuring no one mistook the message in the brutality. Which meant...

He couldn't kill Rannock. Not for avenging his mate.

His Triad lived by a code. He and his brothers never killed without good reason. His conscience refused to let him. Toss in a rigid sense of fairness in all things, and, sad to say, his fight with Rannock was destined to be one-sided. No magic could be used. He must sheathe his usual weapons, play fair and resist the urge to unleash the full extent of his power while giving Rannock the fight he craved.

A brutal one.

Nothing else would settle his scales. The dragon warrior needed to satisfy his pride and soothe primal instincts. Whether he knew it or not, Rannock wanted to prove to his mate—and himself—he could protect her, even in the face of overwhelming odds.

Pushing away from the wall, Rathbone cracked his knuckles. "Fists, no weapons."

"Agreed," Rannock growled, moving with unnatural speed.

A heavy fist broke through Rathbone's guard.

Knuckles cracked against his cheekbone. His head snapped to the side. Blood washed into his mouth. He shifted right, unwrapping a roundhouse beneath the male's chin. Rannock grunted, stumbling backward.

Rathbone grinned, feeling more alive than he had in months, maybe years, as he and Rannock circled each other.

The warrior struck.

Rathbone parried, taking punches, landing some of his own.

A cut opened over his eyebrow. Blood trickling down his face, he blocked a punch, then spun to deliver one of his own. A mistake. Rathbone knew it the second he moved. Rannock was too strong. An expert in hand-to-hand combat, the warrior showed no mercy, moving Rathbone where he wanted him to go, allowing him to gain ground, only to take it away.

A series of hollow victories. A brutal lesson in humility.

Heart racing, chest heaving, Rathbone tried a counterattack. Grabbing his forearm, Rannock kicked the side of his leg. His knee buckled. As he cursed, the dragon warrior drove him backward, toward the staircase. His feet slid toward the top step. He teetered on the edge a second, then lowered his head and lunged at Rannock. His shoulder rammed into the male's chest.

Surprised by the move, Rannock spun around and slammed into the banister. Wood splintered. The heavy post gave way. Rathbone lost his footing. Momentum took over, throwing him into the yawning mouth of the stairwell. He heard Rannock curse a second before the male followed him over the edge, tumbling down the stairs behind him.

26

Yanking the door open, Cate raced into the hall just in time to see Rannock fall down the stairs. She heard the scramble and bang as he slammed down the stone steps. Her breath caught. Shock spun into fear. Alarm compressed her chest, making it hard to breathe as she stood frozen in the middle of the corridor, listening to him tumble.

A thump, then another, rumbled up the staircase. The awful cacophony spiraled against the high ceiling. Wall sconces rattled as the floor under her feet shook.

"Shit," she whispered, afraid to move, afraid to look, afraid she'd discover—

A door opened behind her.

A low growl rolled into the hallway. "What the hell's going on?"

Flinching, she glanced over her shoulder. Blond hair messy from sleep, eyes fierce, Levin prowled into the corridor. Further down, two doors whipped open. A pair of guys exited. Both dark-haired, huge, and wearing angry looks on ridiculously handsome faces.

Getting a load of her expression, Levin held his

hand up. The pissed-off pair stopped short behind him.

His brow furrowed, Levin tipped his chin. "Cate?"

Breathing hard, she swallowed, then went searching for her voice. "Rannock's trying to kill Rathbone."

"Righteous." Eerie yellow eyes trained on her, the first guy smiled.

"About time," the second guy muttered.

"Of course he is," Levin said at the same time, sounding pleased and somehow casual, as though killing people wasn't unusual. Nothing but another day in the life of dragons. "The bastard deserves it, lass. Best tae leave Ran tae it."

She pointed toward the broken railing. "He fell down the stairs."

"A few broken bones willnae stop him."

"Thank fuck," the other guy said, American accent prevalent amidst the Scottish brogues. "Rathbone needs to bleed."

A string of curses drifted up the staircase.

Horrified, she looked at the trio staring back at her. "Are you crazy?"

Three sets of brows popped skyward.

She huffed. "I mean... seriously? You're not going to help him?"

Levin shook his head. "Four against one. Not verra sporting, lass."

"But..." Heart beating triple-time, she forced herself to calm down. Logic, reason, a proper argument—she needed to employ all three if she wanted Rannock's packmates to move. "You have no idea. Rathbone is... he's..."

She waved her hands around. "With the lightning

stuff and the weird lion snake thing... You guys, Rannock could get hurt."

The first guy snorted.

The American guy scoffed.

Levin looked at her as though she'd lost her mind.

In truth, it was a distinct possibility and... shit. So much for the proper use of logic.

She'd bungled the explanation, sounding as insane as she felt. Then again, Cate figured she was justified. The last forty-eight hours had thrown one bad thing after another at her. No time to catch her breath. Zero chance to acclimatize. The only good thing about the situation started and ended with Rannock, her dragon, the one person made and meant for her. The guy she'd dreamed of meeting before she knew what true love really meant, how much it mattered, or the lengths she'd go to protect it.

Fisting her hands, she glared at the jerks trying to convince her to be unconcerned. "Well, if you won't help, I will."

She spun on her heel.

"Lass," Levin said, a warning in his tone.

"Screw you, Lev," she said, using Rannock's nickname for him, running toward the lip of the stairs.

"And she's off," the American said, sounding amused. "Look at her go, Tempel. She's quick."

Levin sighed. "So bloody headstrong. Just like her sister."

Someone chuckled. "The best ones always are."

Ignoring the idiotic by-play, Cate didn't bother to correct the jerks. Nor did she look back. Reaching the top step, she plunged into the gloom. Feet hammering stone treads, she raced down the stairs.

Heavy footfalls sounded behind her.

A horrendous crash echoed from down below.

Shadows grew thicker as the wide spiral staircase curved. No line of sight. Little light to go by. Instinct warned her to slow down. Cate refused to comply. Something beyond the obvious was wrong. She couldn't hear Rannock anymore. The sound of fighting had stopped. No more cursing drifted up from downstairs.

Alarm skittered down her spine. Fear made her pick up the pace. Moving too fast in too little light, she gripped the handrail and kept running.

Levin cursed behind her. "Cate! Slow down. There's—"

"Ran!" she shouted, hurtling down another flight. Her foot caught on something.

Debris pinballed underfoot. Metal shrieked over stone, tripping her up. A moment later, she was airborne, tumbling out of control, falling into the jagged jaws of darkness.

27

Both fists raised, Rannock dodged another punch. Up on the balls of his feet, he spun to his left. Precise footwork. Perfect balance. His combat boots slid across the thick area rug, avoiding the debris scattered underfoot as he waited for an opening. Halfway through the spin, Rathbone let down his guard.

Rannock struck fast. Bone cracked against bone as he hammered the male. Again. For the...

Shite. He didn't know. He'd lost count after hitting the bastard for the third time. Had to give him credit, though—tenacious to a fault, Rathbone refused to back down, countering with a combination.

Jab. Left cross. Uppercut.

Not a bad move.

A less skilled fighter would've fallen for the duck-and-cover, been fooled by the quick shift, and nailed in the ensuing confusion. Not Rannock. The Shadow Walker had skill and speed, but Rannock possessed that plus brute force. Considered a heavyweight by his kind, he was a powerhouse in and out of dragon form. Comfortable with violence, accustomed to delivering it, and showing no mercy when he did.

A lifetime spent sparring with his brothers-in-arms had taught him well. Anyone with enough balls to challenge Rannock paid the price. Usually with a trip to the medial clinic to get stitched up.

Kind of unfair, when he thought about it.

Rathbone didn't stand a chance. Not that he was a bad fighter, simply untrained and rusty. A lethal combination, one Rannock exploited over and over again. Picking his moments. Hitting the male where it hurt most. Humbling the arrogant prick one powerful punch at a time.

Blocking another strike, Rannock slammed his fist into the male's side.

Rathbone cursed.

He nailed him again—same spot, harder blow.

A rasp exploded from the Shadow Walker's throat. He swung blindly. Rannock danced out of reach, then waited for the male to turn. The instant Rathbone swiveled, Rannock hammered him with his elbow. Hard bone cracked against vulnerable temple. Rathbone's head snapped to the side. A cut opened below his eye. The metallic tang of blood suffused the air. Done playing, Rannock moved in for the kill.

Time to end it.

He'd made his point, avenged his female, and exorcised his rage, along with a few demons. Nothing good would come from finishing Rathbone. Despite their differences, the Shadow Walker occupied rarefied air among Magickind. Much as it pained Rannock to admit, the planet needed more of the bastards, not fewer, to heal and recover—to unravel the mess humans continued to make of the environment.

With a growl, Rannock kicked the male's feet out from under him.

Rathbone hit his knees.

Sliding left, he slipped his arm under, then over Rathbone's shoulder. He tightened his grip, pinning the male in a half nelson.

Breathing hard, Rathbone bucked. Blood flew, arching off his face, splattering across the floor.

"Stop fighting, lad. We're done."

"Thought you wanted to kill me."

"Started out that way."

Chest heaving, the male shuddered. "What changed?"

"You've got skill, Rathbone," he said, deflecting to avoid admitting the truth. The bastard didn't need to know his thoughts on the matter... or the fact he understood how important the Triad was to Dragonkind's continued good health. "But you're raw. Untrained. No real challenge for me in hand-to-hand."

"Fuck." Still struggling, Rathbone grabbed Rannock's wrist and pulled, trying to break free. "Who trained you?"

"Got brothers too. Brutal bastards who try tae beat the shite out of me on a regular basis."

"I understand the impulse."

He huffed in amusement.

Rathbone growled. "Let go, asshole."

"Easy," he murmured, loosening his grip. "Donnae—"

"Ran!"

Full of fear, Cate's voice echoed down from above. Fast footfalls followed, plunging into the unlit stairwell.

Shoving Rathbone aside, Rannock pivoted toward the stairs. Wood splinters skated over stone. Metal clanged. She sucked in a harsh breath. He yelled a sharp command.

Flames on candle wicks flared. Light spilled,

casting shadows as Cate tripped over a piece of broken railing, tumbling arse over heels toward the bottom on the stairs.

He reacted, moving to intercept her. Throwing out his hand, he conjured a thick web. Cate somersaulted into the netting. The material dipped, then flexed, tossing her toward the ceiling.

"Shit!" she yelled, arms and legs flailing.

"Jesus," Rathbone muttered, struggling to his feet.

Sliding to a stop beneath her, Rannock watched her go up. She started to come down. Prepared to catch her, timing it just right, he raised his arms. She landed with a thump against him. Out of breath, heart hammering like a runaway drum, she stared at him with big blue eyes. Suffering from shock, she opened her mouth to say something, then closed it again.

"*Bellmia*?"

"Holy crap," she rasped, trying to catch her breath. "It was too quiet. I thought you were hurt. I thought he—"

"Nay."

"—used his lightning whip and just..." She looked him over, searching for injuries.

Mouth pressed to her temple, he let her touch, enjoying the feel of her in his arms. "Lightning whip, lass?"

Checking the back of his head for blood, she nodded. "When Dillinger attacked me, he—"

He snarled. "Dillinger attacked you?"

Cate blinked. "Only a little. He didn't do any serious damage. Couple of scratches. Some bruises. Nothing to worry—"

"What the fuck?" Teeth clenched, he spun to glare at Rathbone.

Cate jolted against him.

The male raised his hands. "The arrival of the Tri-Hexe forced him to shift into one of his forms. Not his fault. He couldn't control it."

Rannock frowned. "One of his forms?"

"The least cooperative one," Cate said with a shrug, treating the occurrence as old news.

"So far," Rathbone murmured, wiping blood from his face with the hem of his tattered dress shirt.

"So far?" Out of breath, Levin slid to a stop beside Rannock.

On his heels, Kruger skidded to a halt on his other side. "Have many forms does the bastard have?"

Rathbone shrugged. "As of yet—undetermined. A new one shows up every once in a while."

"Interesting," Tempel said, trotting down the last few steps. "Give me a blood sample, and I might be able to figure it out."

"Let me guess." Pale gaze riveted to Tempel, Rathbone raised a brow. "Earth dragon. Skilled at deciphering DNA sequences of plants and animals."

Tempel nodded.

"Thanks, but I think my brother'll give your scan a hard pass."

"Offer stands." Hands in his pockets, Tempel sauntered down the hall like he had all the time in the world. Deception at its best, lethal urges well hidden. After what happened to his former pack in Belarus, the male was rarely, if ever, relaxed. Stepping over a downed suit of armor scattered across the area rug, he stopped next to Rathbone. Far enough away to remain respectful, close enough to intimidate. "Now, can we talk about the elephant in the room?"

"My dad," Cate said, shifting in his arms, asking without words to be put down.

Rannock complied, dropping her feet to the foot.

As her boots touched down, he pulled her close, keeping his arm around her.

"Where is he, Rathbone?" she asked, taking control of the conversation.

Her right.

Only fair.

Cate's sire, her rules... until he deemed it necessary to step in and protect her.

"It's not good news, Cate," Rathbone said, expression guarded, tone reserved. "When Rannock and his brothers brought your sire in, he was in bad shape. Suffering from magic sickness. Worse case I've ever seen."

"What does that mean?"

"It's like severe radiation poisoning. No one survives that kind of infection. Magic sickness in humans has a one hundred percent mortality rate."

"What..." Shaking her head, Cate cleared her throat. "What are you saying? That he's... that h-he..."

"I'm sorry," Rathbone said softly. "He passed away early this morning. There was nothing we could do."

"No. No. That's not right. It can't be right." She looked at Rannock, hoping he'd refute the truth.

"Catie-mine," he whispered, hurting for her.

"No, Ran. He can't be dead," she said, voice gone hoarse. A tremor rippled through her. "It doesn't make sense. He's my dad. Larger than life. He knows what jobs to stay away from. Even when things go bad, he finds a way out. He's a master at getting out of sketchy situations. The best. The absolute *best*."

Hating to see her struggle, he cupped her cheek. "Lass."

She shook her head. "He can't be gone. He just can't be, Ran. He knows. My dad knows how to get away."

Rathbone murmured, "He's gone, honey."

"Can I see him?" she asked. "Can I—"

"Nay, you cannae, Cate," he said, despising himself for denying her. A hard pill to swallow, but no matter how painful, he refused to lie to his mate. Cate needed his honesty. She deserved the truth, even if it meant delivering another blow and watching tears fill her eyes. "I'm sorry, lass, but he's contaminated by witchling black magic. You cannae get anywhere near him without becoming infected."

Air rasped in her throat. Her voice broke on a denial.

His heart followed suit, shattering as he watched her absorb the blow. Disbelief turned to pain. Her eyes reflected the shift as her expression crumbled and emotion swelled. Stark agony. Deep sorrow. Gut-wrenching guilt. Connected to her, he felt the brutal combination grab hold and sink its claws deep. She made a hoarse sound as the first tear fell.

She sobbed his name.

Wrapping both arms around her, Rannock hugged her tighter. As she burrowed in, he murmured, trying to soothe her even though he knew he couldn't. Grief went its own way, carving out different paths for different people. After the loses he'd suffered, he knew that better than most. And so when her knees buckled, he didn't prevent her from falling. He folded with her, taking her with him to the floor, pulling her into his lap, doing the only she needed him to do in the moment—hold her together while grief tore her apart.

28

Standing in front of her father's grave, Cate choked back another round of tears. No one needed to hear her cry again. Least of all her. But even as emotion clogged her throat, she found gratitude in the midst of terrible grief.

She wasn't alone in the cemetery.

Rannock stood at her back less than ten feet away, standing strong beneath live oaks dripping with Spanish moss, silent and supportive while she said her goodbyes. Giving her space. Staying close in case she needed him. Guarding her solitude while dragon warriors patrolled the perimeter.

The trees swayed as one flew overhead. A whisper upon the breeze.

Stark relief filled her as her eyes closed. A fanciful thought. Nothing but her imagination. Dragonkind never flew in open skies without being cloaked by an invisibility spell. Cate knew it even as she took comfort in the pack's protectiveness.

Something about being watched over soothed her.

Most people would dislike the idea. But after years spent mired in uncertainty, Rannock and his friends' solid presence reached places deep inside her. Wounded places. Tortured places. Places she revisited tonight as she stared at her dad's gravestone.

Pale marble with a simple inscription. Her dad's name and a dash between two dates.

A gift from Rathbone and his brothers, along with the burial plot. How the Shadow Walker pulled it together so quickly, Cate didn't know. She hadn't asked. Numb from shock, deep in grief, she said *thank you* instead of questioning his generosity.

Knowing what she needed, Rannock hadn't objected. He nodded instead, approving of the Triad's thoughtfulness.

Something else to be grateful for in the midst of a nightmare.

Her throat went tight. An uncooperative tear fell.

She wiped it away, grounding herself in the here and now—in the soil in which she stood. Hallowed ground. The final resting place of so many over hundreds of years. The last place her father would ever visit.

Closed for the night, the graveyard lay quiet. No footfalls tapping along the stone pathways rising between tall headstones. No tourists murmuring in front of the many statues that stood watch over the cemetery. No one marveling at the tranquility to be found inside a home of the dead.

Crouching down, Cate set her hand on the fresh mound of dirt. She curled her fingers in the loose soil and swallowed the pain, determined to say what she must to a man she'd loved, but never understood.

"Goodbye, Dad," she whispered, wiping another tear away. "It wasn't always a fun ride, but you made it interesting. I would never have become who I am without you. Thank you for making me strong. I get my resilience from you. My street smarts and stubbornness, too. You did the best you could, were the best father you knew how to be, and I honor you for that. Niki would too, if she was here."

Unclenching her fist, Cate smoothed her hand over dimpled soil. "Rest well. Be at peace. I miss you. I'll miss you forever. I love you, Dad."

Her quiet words drifted as insects buzzed, visiting bright flowers resting in their beds. Great oaks swayed above her head. The distant call of an owl echoed. Cate reached out and touched the headstone. Cool marble scraping against her fingertips, she traced her father's name—Henry Biscayne—then pushed to her feet.

As she turned away from the grave, Rannock moved toward her. His boots crunched over gravel. He didn't ask if she was all right. Her mate already knew she wasn't, and wouldn't be for a while. Understanding what she needed, he didn't use words to comfort her. He used actions instead, reaching out, gathering her up, putting her back together, piece by broken piece, in the warmth of his embrace.

His compassion enveloped her.

Cate sighed as her eyes drifted closed. Snug and secure in his arms, she relaxed into him, giving him everything. Her love and acceptance. Her rage and grief. Past hurts, her sorrow-filled present along with every moment of her future, accepting the solace he offered without question.

Her dragon. Her lifeline. The only port in her storm.

Rannock had been that and more from the beginning. The moment she'd heard his voice over the line, she knew her life had change for the better.

Surrounded by his scent, she pressed her cheek to his chest. "Thank you."

"For what?" he said quietly, matching the mood of the cemetery.

"Living up to the promise of your voice. Being my everything."

"*Bellmia*," he murmured, stroking her back, each caress a balm to her wounded soul. "You are a wonder. The privilege is, and will always be, mine."

Standing at her father's grave with his arms around her, he set his cheek against the top of her head. The message was clear—no rush. Rannock had all the time in the world for her.

Minutes ticked into more. Leaves rustled. Damp breezes drifted through the garden cemetery and around them. Her troubled mind settled, allowing her to take a full breath, the first deep one since being told her father was gone.

Giving Rannock a squeeze, she shifted in his arms. "Ready?"

"Whenever you are, lass."

"He's at rest now, Ran. Can't fix it. Can't change it. Nothing more I can do for him now," she said, feeling the lump return to her throat. "Time to go home. I need to hug my sister."

"As you wish, *Bellmia*."

As she wished.

Her dragon's answer to everything. He considered himself fortunate to have found her, but as he took her hand and led her out of the cemetery, Cate knew the truth. She was the lucky one, and always would be.

29

ABERDEEN, SCOTLAND — TWO WEEKS LATER

Planted in the middle of his bed, resting on one elbow, Rannock trailed his fingers down his mate's back. Soft light spilled from the bedside lamp, highlighting the delicate length of her spine. He changed course, tracing her waist before sliding over her lower back.

He drew gentle circles with his fingertips.

A hum of pleasure left his throat.

Such smooth skin. So many intriguing curves and hollows to explore. The beauty of a warm, well-loved female. One who adored being in his bed. One he loved having there every day.

Lying belly-down on his sheets, Cate murmured as he caressed her again. He drew his fingers over the swell of her arse. A sensitive area for her, one he now knew by heart. Teasing her, he drifted over the crease, then dipped his hand between her thighs. He stroked gently, playing without adding any pressure.

Toes curled, her heels kicked up.

She turned her head on the pillow. "You're killing me."

He chuckled. "Wasn't me that kept us up all day, lass."

"Well," she said, tucking her chin into her shoulder. "You're hot, and I was in the mood to explore."

"I hope the mood strikes you often."

"You give me free rein, you might not get any sleep."

"I'm happy tae live in a constant state of sleep deprivation."

Her eyes crinkled at the corners.

Stretched out alongside her, he dipped his head. His lips brushed the back of her shoulder. He kissed her softly, then moved to her temple. "It's after midnight."

"Yeah?"

"Uh-hmm." Smoothing his hand up her back, he slid his fingers into her hair. He played in the shorter strands, enjoying its softness and the scent of her shampoo, something sweet with a touch of tartness. Just like her. Mouth drifting over her cheekbone, he breathed her in, taking her deep inside him. "Happy birthday, Catie-mine."

She smiled. "Feels sweet."

"What?"

"Getting to spend it with you," she murmured, turning him inside out with her honesty.

His mate—always the same, never afraid to lay herself bare and share how she felt about him... or anything else, for that matter. Her bravery floored him. The love shining in her gaze humbled him.

Shifting onto her side, Cate hooked her knee over his hip and wiggled closer. "Are you going to sing *Happy Birthday* to me?"

He huffed.

Her eyebrows rose. "No?"

"Keep dreaming, lass."

Her smile turned into a grin.

"I have something better, though."

"A gift?"

"Aye."

"What kind?"

"The best kind."

"Do I get any clues?"

He shook his head.

She pursed her lips. Planting her small hand on his shoulder, Cate gave him a push. He complied, rolling onto his back. She settled astride him, baring her body, treating him to the loveliest of shows. Enjoying the view, he cupped her breasts.

She set her hands on the back of his and pressed, stilling his caresses. "Don't distract me, Ran. I'm on the hunt. In the chase. Whad'ya get me?"

"You'll have tae get dressed for me tae show you."

Her knees bounced on the mattress. A second later, she vaulted off his hips. He grunted as she dismounted. She landed beside the bed like a gymnast, all lithe grace and little-kid excitement. Grinning ear-to-ear, she danced around the bed, picking through the discarded clothes littering the floor.

She yanked on a pair of sweatpants. Shoving her arms through a long-sleeved tee, she whipped it over her head, went after a hoodie, then hopped over the footboard and jumped onto the bed. Tall wooden bedposts creaked in protest.

Rannock stared at her in wonder.

"Come on, Ran," she said, throwing the covers aside. "No one's ever given me a gift before."

He frowned. "No one?"

She nibbled on her bottom lip. "Well, except for Niki, but she's my sister and that doesn't count." Her brow furrowed. "I mean, it counts, but... Oh, you know what I mean! Ran—get up!"

His lips twitched as she tried to drag him out of bed.

"Ran!"

"Kiss me first, Cate."

Crawling over him, she brushed her lips over his. Her tongue flicked the corner of his mouth. With a growl, he wrapped her up and rolled, reversing their position. She smiled against his mouth. He took the kiss deeper, tangling his tongue with hers, tasting her deep, knowing he'd never get enough of her.

She hummed.

He broke the kiss and rolled again, taking her with him over the edge of the mattress. The second his feet hit the floor, he conjured his clothes. Wearing gray sweats and his favorite Black Sabbath T-shirt, he laced his running shoes up with a thought, then glanced down at his mate.

"Shoes, lass."

"Right," she said, hopping sideways. Wiggling her feet into black flip-flops with three white stripes over the toes, she raced back to his side. Bouncing on the tips of her toes, she declared, "Ready!"

Shaking his head at her antics, he grabbed her hand and, skirting an armchair, towed her across the room. He murmured. His bedroom door unlocked, then swung wide. Crossing the threshold, he turned left toward the rear entrance instead of right, avoiding the common room and kitchen, two places his pack congregated every night. Given the hour—and the rumble of voices drifting up the hallway—Rannock knew his brothers-in-arms were already gathering.

Later would be soon enough to share her.

He wanted Cate to himself for a while. Just him and her. No one else around as he helped her celebrate her birthday in style.

Both hands wrapped around his, Cate walked beside him, following where he led, excitement in each step. The clip-clop of her footwear echoed against the high ceiling. Energized by her enthusiasm, he smiled at her, then turned left at the end of the corridor.

An archway flared into beginnings of a staircase. Nothing fancy. Square construction. Concrete treads. Steel railings bolted to rough stone walls.

Fingers laced with his mate's, Rannock began his descent. His footsteps, accompanied by a loud flip-flopping, bounced around the enclosed space.

"How far down?" Cate asked.

"Three stories."

"Cool."

"Wait until you see it."

She nodded.

He kissed the back of her hand and rounded the last landing. Hand-carved by a master carpenter, a wooden door stood at the bottom of the stairs.

He flicked his fingers. Triple deadbolts slid open.

Without breaking stride, he stepped off the last tread and pushed the heavy panel open. Motion sensors picked up his movement. Lights flipped on, illuminating the huge hangar he housed the projects he worked on—the old helicopters he liked to rip apart and put back together.

Connected to the main lair, but not a part of it, the secluded space acted like a sanctuary, allowing him to retreat into a world of his own making. He worked out a lot of his frustrations by ripping things apart, letting his love of human machines out to play by improving upon the designs.

Far from humans and the clamor aboveground, his hangar was where he came whenever he needed a break from the Dragon's Horn, the resto-pub and

Scotch distillery he owned with his brothers-in-arms. A private place. A space he'd added to, perfecting over time. A workshop he planned to share with his mate, if she wanted to keep working.

"Wow," Cate said, voice echoing under the cavernous dome.

Watching her reaction, Rannock experienced the hangar through her eyes. Smooth concrete floors. Walls carved from pale granite. A soaring ceiling. Six spacious workstations with long stainless-steel surfaces for repairing complex machinery. A dozen standing toolboxes. Mechanical parts stored on shelves in one area, helicopter tires, turbo engines, and rotor blades in another.

At the far end stood the lift he used to raise and lower helicopters into the courtyard behind the distillery. His favorite, the Hog, sat on the tarmac. Huge steel doors that slid open at the touch of a lever sat above it, for liftoff and setting down after he'd taken his baby out for a fly.

Everything in its place. Nothing to mar his setup.

Though he now owned a new section, something he'd worked hard to keep from Cate over the last couple of weeks. Not an easy proposition. A curious lass, she'd wanted to see his workspace. He'd kept putting her off, determined to keep his latest project under wraps until he was ready to reveal it to her.

Walking her down the line, he stopped in front of an area sectioned off by a thick rubberized curtain.

She glanced at him. "This is what you've been working on."

"Aye."

"For me," she said, voice a little hoarse.

"For you." Grabbing the rope hanging from the ceiling, he yanked.

The curtain came down, snapping against the concrete floor, revealing a brand-new area carved into granite. Shiny new worktables. Gleaming red standing toolboxes against the back wall. A customized two-post lift, designed to raise and lower cars. And parked in front of it, three long-neglected classics. A rusted-out Jaguar E-Type convertible with a torn top, a brutalized Aston Martin DB5, and a Fiat Dino coupe with missing quarter panels. All classics. All beat to shit. All vehicles he thought his mate would enjoy taking from trash to treasure.

Cate liked a challenge. He'd given her one in the hopes she'd create her own business, instead of working for someone else.

"Holy crap," Cate rasped, small hand trembling in his.

He gave her a squeeze. "Happy birthday, lass."

Tears in her eyes, she shook free of his hold and threw her arms around him. "Thank you, Ran. Best present ever. I love it, and I love you. You're the absolute best."

"Love you too, Catie-mine."

Wrapping his arms around her, Rannock smiled against the top of her head. Mission accomplished. He'd done his job. His mate was happy, well on her way to healing from the loss of her sire and making his home her own.

Thankfulness streamed through him.

Pleasure followed as Cate laughed, lighting him up, filling his heart to the brim, giving him more in that moment than he'd ever be able to give her in return. She was sunshine and joy, the light of his life, all things bright and beautiful. His one. His only. Now, and in the future.

Tipping her head back, Cate grinned up at him.

He smiled back, so bloody glad he'd picked up the phone. An accident in the beginning. His lifeline in the end. Nothing compared to holding her in his arms, making him wonder why he'd ever doubted his decision. Taking her call was, far and away, the best thing he'd ever done.

EPILOGUE

HENRY

Bonaventure Cemetery - Savannah, Georgia

He woke up in the dark, inside a box filled with nothing but cold. Surrounded by the smell of damp earth and Fae magic.

He recognized the scent. Knew it infused his muscles, drilling down deep to reach his bones.

Twitching, Henry Biscayne drew a sharp breath. His empty chest expanded. Inhuman power filled the void, then surged through his veins. Agonizing sensation coursed through him. His body sparked. His synapses fired. His gaze began to glow like twin spotlights, filling the lead-lined coffin with brilliant blue light.

With a snarl, he punched through thick metal to reach wood. The mahogany shell shattered. His hand met loose soil on the other side. Curling his fingers around the torn edge, he ripped the curved top above him wide open. Soil poured in through the hole. He thrashed, digging through heavy dirt, tunneling up and out.

Cool night air rushed over his arm.

His head broke the surface of the earth.

Clawing his way free, bare skin covered in slick ooze and dirt, he stood next to a gravestone with his name on it. Pale marble. No inscription. Just dates that didn't mean anything.

Turning away from the place the Shadow Walkers tried to kill him, Henry tipped his head back. Eyes closed, he absorbed the faint light pushing through thick tree limbs, then bared his fangs and howled at the moon.

ACKNOWLEDGMENTS

Each book I write challenges me in different ways. FURY OF ISOLATION took me on a wild ride, showing me new things, opening up more mysteries, making me curious about worlds beyond the one Dragonkind inhabits. I love Rannock and Cate for many reasons—their unbreakable bond first among them—but their journey took me on one of my own, introducing me to a Triad of Shadow Walkers for the first time. A group I know I'll be writing about in the future.

I want to thank each and every one of you (my fabulous readers) for following me into the wild and wonderful world inside FURY OF ISOLATION. I hope you had as much fun reading Rannock and Cate's story as I did writing it.

A huge shout-out to my fabulous literary agent, Christine Witthohn. You've always believed in me. I'll love you forever. It's been such fun, and a great privilege, working with you. Here's to many more years to come!

Thanks as well to Tanya and the wonderful team at Oliver Heber Books. I learn more every day working with you. I'm so grateful to be part of your crew.

To my family—you're the best. I love you more than words can express. Thank you for all your love and support. I couldn't do any of it without you.

A NOTE FROM THE AUTHOR

Thank you for taking the time to read Fury of Isolation. If you enjoyed it, please help others find my books so they can enjoy them too.

Recommend it: Please help other readers find this book by recommending it to friends, readers' groups, and discussion boards.

Review it: Let other readers know what you liked or didn't like about Fury of Isolation.

Follow me on Facebook, Instagram and Bookbub to get all the latest news.

Sign up for my Newsletter and get exclusive VIP giveaways, freebies and sales throughout the year.

Book updates can be found at www.CoreeneCallahan.com

Thanks again for taking the time to read my books! You make it all possible, and I am truly grateful.

ALSO BY COREENE CALLAHAN

Dragonfury Scotland

Fury of a Highland Dragon

Fury of Shadows

Fury of Denial

Fury of Persuasion

"Villains" of the Dragonfury Series

Fury of Fate

Fury of Conviction

Dragonfury Series

Fury of Fire

Fury of Ice

Fury of Seduction

Fury of Desire

Fury of Obsession

Fury of Surrender

Fury of Destruction

Circle of Seven Series

Knight Awakened

Knight Avenged

Warriors of the Realm Series

Warrior's Revenge

ABOUT THE AUTHOR

Coreene Callahan is the bestselling author of the Dragonfury Novels and Circle of Seven Series, in which she combines her love of romance and adventure with her passion for history. After graduating with honors in psychology and taking a detour to work in interior design, Coreene returned to her first love: writing. Her debut novel, *Fury of Fire*, was a finalist in the New Jersey Romance Writers Golden Leaf Contest in two categories: Best First Book and Best Paranormal. She lives in Canada with her family, a spirited Anatolian Shepherd, and her wild imaginary world.